Skinny Island

Also by Louis Auchincloss

FICTION

The Indifferent Children
The Injustice Collectors
Sybil
A Law for the Lion
The Romantic Egoists
The Great World and Timothy Colt
Venus in Sparta
Pursuit of the Prodigal
The House of Five Talents
Portrait in Brownstone
Powers of Attorney
The Rector of Justin
The Embezzler
Tales of Manhattan
A World of Profit
Second Chance
I Come as a Thief
The Partners
The Winthrop Covenant
The Dark Lady
The Country Cousin
The House of the Prophet
The Cat and the King
Watchfires
Narcissa and Other Fables
Exit Lady Masham
The Book Class
Honorable Men
Diary of a Yuppie

NONFICTION

Reflections of a Jacobite
Pioneers and Caretakers
Motiveless Malignity
Edith Wharton
Richelieu
A Writer's Capital
Reading Henry James
Life, Law and Letters
Persons of Consequence: Queen Victoria
and Her Circle
False Dawn: Women in the
Age of the Sun King

Skinny Island

More Tales of Manhattan

LOUIS AUCHINCLOSS

Houghton Mifflin Company

BOSTON

1987

Library of Congress Cataloging-in-Publication Data

Auchincloss, Louis.
Skinny island.
Contents: A diary of old New York — The stations
of the cross — The wedding guest — [etc.]
1. Manhattan (New York, N.Y.) — Fiction.   2. New York
(N.Y.) — Fiction.   I. Title.
PS3501.U25S5   1987   813'.54   86-21100
ISBN 0-395-43295-2

Printed in the United States of America

S 10 9 8 7 6 5 4 3 2 1

For

PAUL GOLINSKI

*with gratitude for twenty years
of friendship and association
in the practice of law*

Contents

◻

Skinny Island

A Diary of
Old New York

I PICK UP my journal with a heavy heart to inscribe
what may be its final pages. When I started it, thirty
years ago exactly, on New Year's Day of 1845, I had the
grandiose ambition of becoming the historiographer of our
young republic. My considerable family connection in Manhattan, my experience in banking and foreign trade and my
ventures into public life, climaxing in a term as lieutenant
governor of the state, were all to have provided vantage
points from which to view and describe the evolution of
our great experiment in democracy. And haven't they? I
have seen riots and battles and terrible urban fires; I have
been friendly with some of our bravest soldiers and noblest
statesmen, and now at the age of seventy-two, only three
years younger than our century, I can look back to a
grandsire who was a friend of John Jay and Hamilton and
forward to a new century that will see America take her
rightful place as the leading nation of the planet. My reader,
if reader I ever have, will surely understand why Adrian
Peltz at one point of his life considered himself uniquely
qualified to be the American Saint-Simon.

But I have lost that faith, and what is more, I have lost it in a single day. I used to mock the classic rule that confined the action of a tragedy to twenty-four hours. How could mighty events be circumscribed in so small a time? Yet now I have seen that this could be true in my own life. Let me set down exactly what happened to me on January first, 1875.

I started my usual round of calls on relatives and friends in midmorning. It would take me from my house in Washington Square as far north as my daughter Agatha's residence on Fifth Avenue and Fifty-seventh Street. By then I should have walked more than two miles, quite enough for a gentleman of my years in icy weather, and Agatha's carriage would take me home in plenty of time for the dinner of the Irving Club.

I sallied forth, smart and trim in my greatcoat with the high fur collar, my stovepipe hat and my cane with the gold handle given me by Hamilton Fish on my seventieth birthday. I turned back, as was my wont, to gaze up for a moment at the third floor window of poor Cecilia's bedroom, from which the brave invalid used to wave farewell to me. For two years now I have kept her chamber just as it was on the day she died. How she used to love those New Year's Day calls before her terrible last illness! I sometimes feel guilty at being so much stronger than most of my contemporaries, but I remind myself that if the good Lord has given me greater robustness in old age, it is because he expects more of me.

Leaving Washington Square to proceed due north up the Avenue does not always strike me as following the course of progress. Of course I have always been one of the first to hail the imagination and ingenuity of our native architects, who have fashioned for our wealthy citizens these magnificent replicas of European palaces and châteaux. All this is no doubt stimulating and enriching, but I cannot suppress a faint whiff of regret as I look back to my own noble square of white wood and red brick, of serene, uniform façades behind which some of our most high-minded citizens have been content to dwell in nobly proportioned, unostentatious comfort. They have been happy to depend more on their high wit and good spirits to impress their neighbors than on Romanesque arches or Minoan columns. But, as my children point out, I am hopelessly old-fashioned.

An early call that day was on my son Philip and his lovely wife, Mary. They live in one third of a Moorish structure on Thirty-third Street, the other two thirds of which is occupied by my daughter-in-law's parents, the Schuyler Clintons. As no family is older New York than the latter, they feel they must be modern, and they are very proud of their hideous gray house with its narrow spooky slits of windows and its stunted minarets for chimneys. A reception was being held in the Clintons' part of the mansion in a clutter of curled and twisted draperies, odd copper appliances, gleaming lanterns and a few incomparably beautiful Persian carpets. But the latter, one could hardly see under the crowd.

Philip has been growing apart from me lately. I suppose I should not resent this. After all, he is forty-seven, and I never dreamed that I would live to have a child so old. It is not that he resents me, certainly not that he is jealous of me, and probably not that he is becoming any less fond of me. It is more as if he were beginning to despair of ever being able to make me comprehend what to him are the obvious facts of life. Philip is as flat as I am exuberant, as dark as I was once blond, though now of course gray. He seems paler these days, and tired.

He and I stood in a corner while I quaffed a glass of punch, as tasty as the house was ugly. Philip drank nothing, explaining that it was going to be a long day. He seemed totally unconcerned with the other guests.

"There's something I think you ought to do for Jake Smull," he said to me suddenly. "It's only a little thing, really. He wants to have the Historical Society put on an exhibit of his project for a fairground in Central Park."

I have made few entries about Jacob Smull in my journal, so perhaps I should pause now to do so. Everyone knows he is the principal owner of the East Coast Railway Line, and most people assume that he is a man of more energy than scruple. Certainly he is a poor shred of flesh to house so big a brain and to hold up such shabby black suits. He has recently acquired a controlling interest in the Standard Trust Company, and I suppose it is generally assumed that, as its president, I have become his puppet. But at least until this last New Year's Day I had not found it so. Smull has been silent and civil at the few board meetings he has attended, and he accepted quite graciously my bid to him to join my dining club, the Irving. I have always considered it the duty of the older members of society to train and take in those newcomers who show promise. After all, the Peltzes themselves are by no means old New York by the standards of the Schuylers and Clintons. My mother's father was an auctioneer and his father a mere carpenter. We started simply, but we have sunk deep roots. It behooves us to help others to do so.

"I see there are a couple of matters that I have to

straighten out, my boy," I said in a kindly paternal tone, laying a hand on Philip's shoulder. "I know that I'm talking to one of the luminaries of the New York bar, but attorneys sometimes wear blinkers where their clients are concerned. Jacob Smull of course is very important to your firm —"

"He's rather important to you, too, Father."

"Yes, yes, dear boy, I'm quite aware of that." I paused to allow any testiness to drain out of my tone. "But you must remember that to a public servant such as I have been — and still, to an extent, continue to be — there are civic obligations that transcend any private interest. I was, after all, one of the original commissioners of Central Park."

"Do you think Jake Smull isn't aware of that? Any more than he isn't aware that you're president of the Historical Society? Why do you think he came to me with his project?"

I smiled patiently. "If Smull thinks I am going to use my public influence for his private advantage, he must be taught differently. Look here, Philip. I don't blame any man for seeking preferential treatment. That's only human. But he should understand when that treatment is refused."

"I'm not sure Smull will."

"Well, that's his concern, isn't it?"

Philip tried to control his impatience. The old man, he was telling himself, had to be handled. "But is this really preferential treatment, sir? It isn't as if Smull were feathering his own nest. His proposed fairground is a public project."

"Oh, Philip. No Wall Street lawyer could be *that* naive. You know as well as I do that Smull is looking at his fairground with just one purpose in mind: a fat profit for Jacob Smull. It's no secret that he is transferring some of his railroad profits into city real estate and concessions. And now that the original commissioners have been kicked off the Park board and replaced by hungry politicians, I suppose our little urban Garden of Eden will be up for grabs. But don't ask Adrian Peltz to contribute to the destruction of his own handiwork!"

"Father, one fairground is hardly going to destroy a park. It may even enhance it."

"Don't you believe it, my boy! It will be a honky-tonk full of old Smull's vulgar sideshows. And that will be just the beginning, too. The poor park will soon be —"

"You don't seem to think too much of your friend Smull," Philip interrupted me. "And haven't you even taken him into your sacred Irving Club?"

"I have," I replied imperturbably. "And I have hopes for him. Jacob Smull has the makings of a gentleman. But he was not bred as such. He has rough corners, craggy edges. It is the duty of our class to educate the new rich in the old ways and manners. Only in that way can society, which is a constantly changing body, hope to maintain its high customs and traditions."

"And you really believe you can educate Jake Smull?"

"I believe there's a chance of it, yes."

"You don't think he's trying to educate *you*? In the ways and means of buccaneers?"

"I disdain to answer that, Philip. But I might point out that you are not speaking with very noticeable loyalty of the principal client of your firm."

"I'm speaking to my *father*," Philip replied in a lower, tenser tone. "If I can't speak candidly to him, to whom can I? Of course, I owe loyalty to Smull. But I also owe loyalty to you. I've got to make you see the kind of man Smull is. You are in his hands, sir!"

"Me?"

"Well, your bank is. Your welfare is. Smull never does anything without a reason, and one of the reasons that he wanted to control Standard Trust was to control its directors."

"He'll find he's bitten off more than he can chew there."

"Father, listen to me." Philip's tone was almost pleading now. "I happen to know that Smull has set his mind on this fairground and that he's counting on that exhibition at the Historical Society. Just as he counted on you to get him into the Irving Club."

"I did that for the reasons I have just described," I retorted.

"But, Father, he doesn't believe that! He believes you're simply dazzled by his money. And that you'll do pretty much anything he reasonably requests of you. And he believes this exhibit is a reasonable request. What difference does one exhibit more or less make to the Historical Society?"

"It makes the difference that it will put the Society in the position of plundering the Park. It will make cannibals of the city's cultural institutions! My answer to Jacob Smull will be a polite but firm negative."

"Father, please! For your own sake!"

"For *my* sake? Isn't it rather for yours? Isn't it for your client that you're arguing now? You speak of your duty to me, but I suggest that you may have a conflict of interests. It even occurs to me now that you may have had the same conflict when you induced me to persuade my board to accept the control of Standard Trust by Mr. Smull. Were you acting in my best interests, sir, or in your client's?"

Philip waxed pale indeed as he clenched his fists. For a moment he could find no words, and when he spoke his voice trembled. "You accuse me of a conflict there? Well, indeed you're right. I *did* have a conflict. I persuaded my client to take over a wobbly bank that might have failed without him. Only I didn't tell him how wobbly it was. I betrayed Jacob Smull for *you*, Father."

I eyed him in disbelief. "You grossly exaggerate the precarious condition of my bank. My only concern is why you are doing so."

Philip looked up at the ceiling as if in appeal to whatever deity might exist among the chandeliers of a Moorish house. "Father, you're living in a fool's paradise. Listen to the prayer of your son. Don't let Jacob Smull turn it into a fool's hell!"

I glared at my unhappy heir. "I can only presume, sir, that you have had a glass too much of your father-in-law's excellent punch. Let me wish you a happy new year!"

Turning to the hall I should have left the party then and there but for the fact that Mary, my lovely daughter-in-law, hurried after me and caught me by the arm.

"Mr. Peltz! You can't go without drinking to the new year with me."

I turned at once back to the punch bowl with dearest Mary, and we each took up a glass.

"I saw you talking to Philip, and you both looked so glum! I'm afraid Philip has been worried about business matters. I'm so relieved you're here. You always put things in their right proportion. You make sense out of the most chaotic messes. When I am with you I believe that the world has a beginning, a middle and an ending. I like that. Oh, dear Mr. Peltz, I like it very much!"

I looked devotedly into those dark, dark eyes and at that concerned, heart-shaped face. "I hope you don't like it too much, my dear. We live in a strange new world."

"Oh, don't say that! Don't *you* say that. That's the way Daddy and Philip talk."

I took her hand to pat it. "Then I shan't, my dear. You and I will show them the way. We'll show them there's not only a future, but a great and noble past. And that it's always with us!"

My daughter, Agatha, was my last visit that day, all the way north on Fifty-seventh Street in the row of French houses that Mary Mason Jones had erected for herself and her lessees. I have never seen the sense in trying to turn our chocolate city into a feeble copy of Paris. It simply emphasizes all the things we haven't got. Agatha went to France in the winter after the terrible *commune* and was able to bring back all sorts of Second Empire furniture, some from Fontainebleau itself. Now her house is full of gilded bees and eagles and odd curlicued chairs whose seats turn on wheels and long narrow divans you can't really sit on. I wonder she doesn't sometimes reflect on the fate of the empire that produced these things.

Agatha has gushing good manners that seem to go with her buxom blondness and the frou-frou of her heavy taffeta dresses, and she always treats me with elaborate respect and affection. But I well know that beneath her demonstrativeness there beats a heart that is the willing slave of her handsome, philandering husband, whose total lack of imagination, sometimes erroneously identified with sound business acumen, has led him into some very bad deals indeed. I feared that the new year was going to bring further troubles when she led me aside from her guests for a private conference.

"Father, I know you'll forgive me for intermeddling in a matter that is, properly speaking, only your affair. But sometimes things come up where I just have to."

"What sort of things, my dear?"

"Well, now, don't get all mad when I tell you it involves your sacred Irving Club."

"I can't ever get all mad at you, silly girl. But I fail to see how you could be very much involved with a gentlemen's small dinner club."

"It's just that I gave a great friend of Charles's the least little reason to believe you might not oppose his membership."

"In other words," I said, smiling, "you promised him my vote. Which in the Irving is still tantamount to his admission. Well, I don't know that's such a terrible crime. Charles knows we need younger members, and I can't imagine where we would rather look for recruits than among the young bloods who make up his circle."

"Except this wouldn't exactly be a young blood."

"Oh? Well, age need not be a total disqualification. *I* am hardly the one to raise it as a bar. Who is this gentleman, pray?"

Agatha paused. "You may be surprised."

"Surprise me then."

"Conroy Morrissey."

I stared and then blinked. "You mean a relative of the judge?"

"I mean the judge himself."

"Agatha, is this a joke? The taste is questionable."

"It's not a joke!" she cried in instant indignation. "Judge Morrissey is putting together a real estate deal that could make our fortune if he'd only include Charles. Oh, Father, you can't spoil it!"

"I know all about Morrissey's real estate deals," I said dryly. "I also know about his congressional record during the war. The man is not only dishonest; he was a Copperhead. He backed McClellan in sixty-four. I could almost prove he was a traitor. And you told him that *I* would favor his admission to the Irving? I wonder he didn't laugh in your face."

"On the contrary, he said he had always been one of your greatest admirers."

"Well, he can continue to admire me from afar. A member of the Irving! Why, even if I could face the scandalized faces of my fellow members, how could I bear the reproachful eyes of your brother Archie's spirit? Or of the three hundred thousand other boys who perished to preserve our union."

"Oh, Father, you and your war. It's always hopeless when you start waving the bloody shirt."

My war! The bloody shirt! In one small decade had all memory of valor departed from the land? I had to be quiet for a moment to keep myself from some unseemly explosion. It was true that my enthusiasm for the Union cause had amounted to a religion — almost, in the eyes of some, to fanaticism. I had perhaps thought too much in terms of the glorious phrases of Mrs. Howe's battle hymn accompanying General Sherman's thrilling march to the sea and too little in terms of the corpses and maimed bodies of our boys in blue. And on occasion I force myself to recall — oh, the bitter memory! — the mild reproach of my darling Archie the first time he was wounded and I rushed to his side in Virginia with a pass from Secretary of War Stanton himself. "Father," he murmured from his bed of pain, "did you stop to think that the men who escorted you to the front may have had to risk their lives?" Which is why I did not go to him after his fatal wounding at Gettysburg and was not there to hold his hand when he died. But whatever my exaggerations, whatever my sentimentalities even, as some might call them, are they not preferable to Agatha's cold indifference to the generation of dead boys that made her ease and opulence possible?

"Some memories will always be sacred to me," I at last limited myself to stating.

"But don't you see, you can't just live in memories?" Agatha demanded. "The world moves on. Archie himself would have seen that. He was always a practical fellow. He and I used to conspire together on how to dress things up when we had something to ask of you that we were afraid you'd refuse."

"Are you implying, Agatha, that Archie, if alive today, would approve of my taking into a club a man who wanted to sell out to secession?"

"All I'm saying is that Archie would have let bygones be bygones. He did enough fighting in the war. He wouldn't have kept it up all his life."

I am afraid that I almost disliked my daughter at that particular moment. Certainly I did not wish to stay another minute under her roof.

That unhappy night we sat down twelve at my board for a dinner meeting of the Irving Club. The dozen men present included two judges, a former governor, a former mayor, the president of Columbia University, Jacob Smull and my son Philip. I thought the dining room with its Duncan Phyfe chairs, its splendid dark mahogany sideboard with the golden eagle claw feet and my great Sully of President Washington had never looked finer. I hoped that it would make a suitable impression on Smull for his first appearance in our midst. It did not.

But nothing would have, as I now sadly see, other than

the promise of a profitable investment. Smull appeared to me that night in the full glare of his singleness of mind and purpose. Perhaps it was the contrast that he afforded to my more richly variegated guests. Small, dry, bald, tight-lipped, he seemed to have shriveled to a mere husk of acquisitiveness. He did not even bother to pretend that it was a gratifying experience to make his maiden appearance in our midst. He spoke in a mild, rather quavering tone that nonetheless had the persistence of a bubbling stream. If it was occasionally lost to louder tones; as soon as the latter subsided, it was heard again.

"If you don't mind my saying so, Governor, you're going to see some rather cloudy skies in this Huntington Beach project. It's all very well for the developers to assume that the potato farmer will welcome the intrusion of additional summer residents, but have they taken into consideration . . . ?"

As the evening wore on my dismay began to identify itself more with my other guests than with Smull. For when other topics were introduced, a novel of Mark Twain's, plans for the new art museum, the plight of the Western bison, an exhibition of Kensett's landscapes, Smull treated them as if they had been so many coughs or sneezes, either keeping a brief silence or else countering with another business question, only perfunctorily related to the subject. And the table went along with him! My distinguished fellow members were like so many choir boys swapping stories, who came to respectful attention when the priest came in to direct their attention to the service. Had I discovered the essence of our civilization? Men will defer to the first in any group who introduces a topic that is recognized as sacred. On an English weekend, over the port, I have seen how quickly the subject is changed, even from politics, to hunting; in France, even from money, to women. With us it seems to be money. Spending it, hoarding it, marrying it, killing for it — all of which strike me as at least human or dramatic subjects — are not in question. Only the making or the increasing of money seems to matter to the true Yankee.

As the evening wore on and I became more and more silent, the small white face of Jacob Smull with its ever-moving pale lips began to seem to me less dull than sinister. He even achieved a kind of dignity, for there were unquestionably aspects of leadership in this sere wisp of a man. He was not, after all, just a grubber for coins; he was in fact a kind of priest, the prelate of an established order, an Inquisitor, a Torquemada, who knew that he did not have to raise his voice or wave his arms to command attention and profound respect.

After dinner he came to sit beside me in the library for a word apart from the others.

"It has been a pleasant evening, Peltz," his flat tone reported. I have never heard him use a Christian name. "It occurred to me that you might like to hear of a gentleman who might appreciate these gatherings. I need not tell you of his distinguished public career. I refer to Judge Morrissey."

I felt a tickling through my veins. I actually smiled at my interlocutor! And then I recognized what was going on in my mind and through my limbs. It was the arrival of an irreversible decision. It was actually a pleasant sensation!

"No, you need not tell me, Smull. I know all about Judge Morrissey's treasonable career. Had he had his way we should now be two nations. And one of them would be a slave state."

My tone was so matter-of-fact that Smull needed a minute to take in my meaning.

"Was it treason to be opposed to Abe Lincoln?"

"I believe so."

"Then you wouldn't consider his candidacy?"

"Never. But you're free, of course, to ask others. I shall simply resign if he's elected."

Smull pursed his lips into a tiny arc. "Well, I guess if it's no club for you with him, it's none for me without him. Good night, Mr. Peltz. Do you need my written resignation?"

"It won't be necessary, Mr. Smull. I'm sorry you feel as you do. We shall continue to meet at board meetings of the bank, I trust."

"For a time, Mr. Peltz."

He did not even have to put a threat in his tone. The words did everything.

There was an atmosphere of relief when Smull had left, and the group now talked about everything under the sun, from the new territory of Alaska to the merit of Walt Whitman's poetry. We were very hearty and drank several bottles of champagne. When all but Philip departed at midnight, I told him of Smull's resignation. He was grim but not surprised.

"He never forgives, you know. He seems impersonal, but he's not. He's vindictive."

"What can he do to me?"

"Kick you out of Standard Trust."

"Haven't I reached an age to retire?"

"Father, what are you going to live on?" There was an agony of concern in Philip's tone, and I recognized with a start that my son still loved me. "You know how much your principal has eroded."

"I do know. I shall sell this house and take a single room in one of the new hotels."

"You! Adrian Peltz!"

"I shall be a free man, Philip."

"I suppose you could always live with me or Agatha."

"I couldn't live with Agatha. You know that. And I'd never impose myself on your darling Mary."

"Father. Dad. Listen to me. That all sounds very brave, but you won't like it when it comes. I had an idea that something like this was going to happen tonight, and I brought a manuscript I want you to read. You know that Mother kept a diary in her last two years, don't you?"

"And that she gave it to you before she died." I nodded gravely. I had been bitterly hurt that she had not entrusted it to me. "To do with as you saw fit. In your absolute discretion. I have honored her wish. I have never even mentioned it to you."

"I know. You have been, as always, the perfect gentleman. But now I am exercising that discretion. I am giving it to you."

I stared. "You think there is something in the diary that will alter my decision about Smull?"

"I hope there may be."

"I shall read it this very night."

"It won't take you very long."

It didn't. The journal covered only two years of Cecilia's life, and each entry was brief; I was able to read it in a couple of hours. I had expected to be emotionally unsettled, and I was, but differently than I had anticipated. I found myself perusing the spidery handwriting with the admiration, at times even the jealousy, of a fellow journalist. For what was truly astonishing was the way in which our town, our whole life, was filtered through the curtains of the writer's sickroom windows. Cecilia had seen more from her chaise longue than I in all my perambulations of Manhattan.

Her glimpses of Washington Square — a reference to a blue sky, a child with a hoop, a beggar, a shaft of winter light along red brick, the toll of a bronze bell — were exquisite.

A russet dawn; a shoulder-shuddering chill. Neighbor Matthews to wed today. Will he go to his office first? And then, at noon, open his gold watch to check the hour, nod, cover his ledger, and rise with that rusty cough? His entry: "Wind north northeast. Snow flurries. S.S. Persia still missing. Married Emily Hadden."

Cousin Laura here. How faded the poor dear! Adrian says she was always so, but now you can't tell what color she first was. Spoke of the admitting doctor at Bellevue where she had her operation. Had she ever had a baby? That stare! "You must have misread my name, sir. It is *Miss* Temple."

The passage that I knew awaited me, the one that had induced Philip to give me the diary, was written only two weeks before my darling expired.

It is leaving Adrian that gives me the greatest pain. Men are such idealists, and he the most of all! I sometimes think that half New York society is in a conspiracy to seem to be what Adrian deems it. Once they have glimpsed the beautiful conception in his mind it seems too terrible to let him even suspect the truth. For if he did, if that bright picture ever dimmed, might not some of their light go out as well? New York may have always been a shabby place, but isn't it a touch less shabby if there's an Adrian Peltz to believe in it? Oh, my darling Adrian, if you could only go first, with all the beauty of your young republic still intact in your nobly conceiving imagination, how patiently would I lie up here until it was time to join you!

I have now written out and reread my account of the events of New Year's Day, 1875. My first plan was the right one. This *is* the place to end my diary.

The Stations
of the Cross

MISS JANE LYLE had continued to occupy the tall stooped brownstone, Number 11 West, on the north side of Fifty-seventh Street between Fifth and Sixth Avenues, ever since the death of her mother a decade before, in 1889. It was not a large house, being of the same size and shape as the others in the block, except, of course, for Mrs. Vanderbilt's version of the Château of Blois at the corner, and it could be comfortably run for the old lady by three Irish maids, though even these would have been a drain on her slender resources had not her four brothers, who had prospered as the American agents for Coats thread, been willing to help out. No. 11, after all, had been the home of the old parents whom their sister, sacrificed in the Victorian tradition, had tended to the end. The male Lyles, cognizant of their obligation, were also glad to provide for their sister's summers with annual bids to their villas in Newport, Narragansett and Bar Harbor.

There was a sentiment among the brothers and their families that Jane's life had been a union of sadness and gallantry. She was pictured as treasuring the memory of young Phineas Howland, killed at Antietam and of holding high the lamp of ancient patriotism in a tarnished modern world. Jane was perfectly willing to accept this tribute. What did it matter that she could not precisely recall the features of Phineas Howland or that he had never definitively proposed to her? No doubt he would have, had he come back from the war. And was it of any significance now that the parents whom Jane had so conscientiously nursed and whom she was supposed still tenderly to miss, had become senile invalids whose demises, within a year of each other, had been a blessed relief? Jane had learned the importance of allowing people to keep the image of oneself that it pleased them to keep.

And, after all, she too had an image of herself; indeed, it was that which floated her soul. She was the spirit and rallying point of the whole Lyle clan, her four brothers and their multitudinous descendants — some sixty of them, including in-laws. It was septuagenarian Aunt Jane whose straight, tall, rather massive figure in dark brown or black, and square, strong-featured face with soberly staring eyes, had become familiar to every denizen of Fifty-seventh Street. It was she who gave the Christmas tree party, who led the singing at family song fests and who maintained the famous "treasure drawer" into which every Lyle descendant under the age of fourteen was entitled to reach and "grab" on a call to the venerable relative. When the good lady appeared on the street on her sedate journey to the park, or to the neighboring house of a sister-in-law, or to the Plaza Presbyterian Church, she provided reassurance in the stability of urban society to the passer-by who might reflect: "Well, so long as we have people like Miss Lyle . . ."

Jane was aware that she was to some extent an actress playing a role, but she did not think that this was either undesirable or uncommon. She had seen her mother play the role of the brave invalid. She had also seen that role become a reality, which had given her confidence in the future of her own chosen part of indomitable old maid. Each passing year provided another layer of protection against any return of the silliness of a youth filled with disappointments both bitter and unrecognized by her family. She had wanted to marry, but had never been sure that she was sufficiently in love, and had finally attributed her lack of assured ardor to a heart lost to the corpse on that Maryland battlefield. She had wanted to write and publish inspired poetry, but her sole appearance in print had been in a slender, paper-bound packet entitled *Sylvan Moods*, paid for by a kind but condescending father. She had wanted, finally, in her late thirties, to go to England and study nursing after the example of Miss Nightingale, but her brothers had persuaded her that a more immediate and pressing duty was to their mother, already afflicted by the mysterious malady that would take so many long years to bring her to the tomb. But now all that was behind her, well behind her — the gushing, the flushing, the hysterical tears, the rushing upstairs to her bedroom, the slamming of doors — now there was calm and sense and no mystery. Everyone knew, including Jane Lyle, just where Jane Lyle stood.

Yet having assurances did not mean that she was averse to an occasional surprise. Having placidity did not mean that she had eschewed all excitement. Jane was looking forward now, with an almost uncomfortable intensity, to a visit from the Reverend Gordon Muir. She was very devoted to this young man, whom she allowed to address her as "Aunt Jane." Gordon was the assistant to the golden-tongued minister of the Plaza Presbyterian Church, and his ardent passion to visit the Holy Sepulcher had inspired

Jane with the still secret and feverishly debated notion of using her small hoarded savings to send him there. But the real motive for this proposed generosity she found more difficult to face, and each time that she caught herself avoiding the mental confrontation, she had to remind herself: "Jane Lyle, don't be an old fool! Why can't you, in the privacy of your own mind, ask yourself if Gordon Muir isn't in love with Mrs. Bullock? If he's not, thank your God. If he is, the trip to Jerusalem might be just the thing he needs to give him the strength of soul to overcome Satan!"

Gordon was a plump, short, pale young man, but he had large lustrous brown eyes and thick blond curly hair that reminded Jane of a cherub. She liked to think of him as a Byronic poet; the intensity of his enthusiasms more than made up for any physical shortcomings. As Mr. Bullock had confided once to Jane: "That young man cares almost too much for God." If this sounded irreverent, Jane could still see what he meant. When Gordon led the congregation in prayer, his eyes tightly closed, his head flung back, he seemed to be almost in a trance. When he loudly sang a hymn, following the choir with Mr. Bullock down the aisle in the processional march, he might have been striding to a martyr's death in the arena. But when he assisted Mrs. Bullock at her tea table this same fervor seemed to emanate from a less spiritual source: the raven hair and sullen black eyes of the pastor's wife, who, incidentally, was just half the pastor's age. Jane might have been willing to attribute her suspicion to what her nephew, Tom, who liked to play the "outrageous Lyle" (another role), called the "erotic daydreaming of the dirty Presbyterian mind," had it not been for a certain complacency in Mrs. Bullock's demeanor.

When Gordon came that day, however, they had an

unexpected discussion so upsetting to Jane that she didn't have the force to reveal to him her plan for his future.

The subject of marriage had come up. Jane, who often sought advice from her ministers on theological subjects, had asked his opinion about a Lyle cousin, a hitherto seemingly unconsolable widow who had just contracted a respectable but surprising second matrimonial alliance with her late husband's business partner and closest friend.

"Will they all three find themselves together in heaven?" Jane wanted to know. "I should think it might be rather embarrassing."

But Gordon was categorical. "There is no marrying or giving in marriage in the next world."

"I know that is believed by many. And in the case I mentioned it may be just as well. But in other cases it might be hard. My brother Adam, for example, and his wife Beth. They are so close, so touchingly dependent on each other. I can hardly bear to think of them as being separated through eternity."

"But they will not be separated!" Gordon exclaimed with what struck Jane as an unwarranted agitation. "They will be very much together. All people who love each other truly will be together. It's simply that there will be no marriage."

Jane frowned. "That doesn't somehow seem quite . . . well, quite proper."

"But, dear Aunt Jane, there's no propriety or impropriety in heaven! There will be no flesh, so how could there be sin? Love, true love, will always be allowed. Between any two souls that wish to unite!"

"But supposing there were, say, two male souls that were attracted to one female soul —"

"There are no sexes in heaven," he interrupted.

"But you talk about love. Love as it exists between my brother and sister-in-law. I don't quite see —"

"We shall all be free to love all!" Gordon leaned forward excitedly in his chair, almost dropping his teacup. "There will be no rivalries, no jealousies, no monopolies. Except that perhaps two souls, which love each other supremely, ineffably, eternally, may be allowed a special kind of union. Which no other soul will take umbrage at. Oh, yes, I like to believe that!"

Jane shook her head dubiously. "I'm not sure how everyone would like that. Suppose, for example, that the soul of a dead wife developed this ineffable love for a soul that wasn't her living husband's soul? How would he feel? I mean the husband, after he died, and found the other two together in heaven?"

"Well, of course, he wouldn't mind because it would be heaven, don't you see? You can't 'mind' things in heaven. And, anyway, Aunt Jane, how otherwise would people like you and me have a chance to be happy?"

"What do you mean, people like you and me?" She marveled at the idea of a common denominator between her dry antiquity and his golden youth.

"Why, unmarried people, of course."

"You, dear boy? But you will certainly marry. And before very long, I should hope."

"Never! I shall never marry!"

Jane was shocked by his vehemence. She changed the subject, but she could not change it in her mind. Could it be that this dear young man was endangering his precious soul with the prospect of a posthumous bliss with Mrs. Bullock? It seemed uncanny, ridiculous, but she could not rid herself of the idea, and she noted grimly, the very next time that she saw Mrs. Bullock, at her sister-in-law Beth's house, that Gordon did not quit the side of the pastor's wife throughout the tea party.

Certainly the Reverend Mr. Bullock did not appear to harbor any suspicion. A vast, hearty, cheerful man, pleasantly proud of his unassailable reputation as a preacher, comfortably adored by all the female members of his congregation, he seemed to take quite for granted that his young assistant should act as a constant equerry to his silent, unfathomable young wife. He might even have insisted on it! Mrs. Bullock was neither easy nor popular, and people wondered why a rich widower should have married her, though she was certainly pretty. She had none of the social qualities needed for the wife of the pastor of so important a congregation; she behaved more like a truculent daughter reluctantly comforming herself to the pattern of a father's life than a consort who had presumably chosen her part with eyes wide open.

There had been no one in whom Jane dared confide, but there was one person whom she thought she could indirectly sound out, her favorite brother, John. A huge man with a large belly who had once been handsome and was now imposing, John had a way of barking out banalities in response to questions he hadn't really listened to, but she knew that if she kept at him he would eventually be sympathetic and even kind. He used to take Jane for walks in Central Park on Sunday afternoons when the weather permitted, and on one such outing she asked.

"Gordon Muir told me an odd thing the other day. He said he would never marry. Why do you suppose an attractive man his age would be so sure of that?"

"Oh, plenty of young bucks are that way. I was myself.

We imagine there's nothing in the world like a man's independence. But then Flora came along and put a stop to that nonsense. Same thing will happen to young Muir. You can bet on it."

"And yet he struck me as being almost passionately sincere."

John did not reply; he was too busy clearing his throat, a serious and noisy business. She waited until he had finished.

"I said he seemed so sincere, John."

"Sincere? Who?"

"Gordon Muir. About never marrying."

"Oh, fiddle. Lot of nonsense. He probably imagines he's sweet on Mrs. Bullock."

Jane was so aghast at this abrupt and casual confirmation of her most dire suspicions that she did not trust herself to say another word on the topic. Back home again, she found herself positively indignant with her favorite brother, and her indignation spread rapidly to all gentlemen of his age and class. It struck her now that they were apt to show a throat-clearing (half belching, really), skin-scratching indifference to all the necessary order of a moral society, that they liked to retreat after dinner to their dark libraries and drink whiskey and brandy out of decanters and tell off-color stories, leaving the drawing room and the ladies and civilization itself to fend for themselves.

At the annual fair held for the benefit of the church in the gymnasium of the Plaza Settlement House Jane had her final confirmation of the threat that she had envisaged to Gordon's soul. She found him, as she feared, seated complacently by the booth at which Mrs. Bullock was rather languidly trying to sell kitchen pots and pans.

"Do you think I could deprive you of Mr. Muir's company for a minute, Mrs. Bullock? There is something I should very much like to ask him."

The pastor's wife's large black eyes met hers with a serene stare behind which Jane, with a sudden jump of her heart, was startled to flare a bold hostility. "Can't you ask him in front of me?"

"I don't know," Jane mumbled, much taken aback. "I don't really think I can."

"Then you have secrets with Mr. Muir?"

"No, not secrets exactly . . ."

"What then?"

"Just . . . just things I can't say in public."

"Am I public? Dear me, what abysses!"

"We have business to discuss," Jane exclaimed, grasping for anything.

"Ah, business." Mrs. Bullock threw up her hands. "When I loft Virginia my daddy told me to expect everything up here to give way to business."

"Not quite everything, Ellie," Gordon put in.

"Yes, everything!" she retorted, almost angrily. "I leave you to Miss Lyle. Shoo! Off with you!"

Jane and Gordon walked to a bench by a wall of the great chamber, apart from the din of the booths. There he indicated that she should take a seat.

"Will this do for our 'business,' Aune Jane?" he asked with a smile.

"Very nicely, thank you. I'm sorry to take you away from your friend, but I have been terribly worried about what you told me of your never marrying. It seemed to me that you might be giving up some happiness on this earth in favor of an imaginary union in the hereafter. Is that really wise, Gordon?"

He did not seem to feel her interest in the least intrusive

or the subject an odd one to be discussed by a young man and an old maid at a church fair. "You misunderstood me. I'm not giving up anything on this earth."

"But I mean," she continued, very much perplexed, "if you had formed an attachment for, say, a lady, who was . . . well, not free . . ." Her voice trailed off. She could not cope with the topic.

"She and I could still have our friendship, couldn't we?"

"You mean what they call a 'platonic' one?"

"Call it what you like. I believe we shouldn't be so afraid of our bodies. I believe that is something that is wrong with our culture. We would not have been given desires if desires were evil."

"But you know what our Lord said. That whosoever looketh on a woman to lust after her —"

"Yes, yes, but he meant the man who *intended* to commit adultery. Not the man who feels a desire but will not give in to it. All that condemnation of what we cannot help feeling is Jansenism or Puritanism, a survival of Old Testament Hebraic hatred of the body. I doubt if it even existed among the Christians of the Roman era. I like to think of that as a pale, clear time when chaste youths and maidens met in grave communion to worship God in gardens secluded from the persecuting eye. There must have been a cheerfulness in their courage, a quiet humor in their conviviality, a high seriousness in their acceptance of both happiness and martyrdom. It must have been the furthest possible thing from those smelly hermits living on locusts in the desert and hurling anathemas!"

Gordon spoke with such fire and eloquence that Jane wondered if he were not rehearsing a sermon. She thought she might have read something not unlike what he was saying in that beautiful novel, *Marius the Epicurean*. But literature was one thing, and playing with fire another.

"Some of those hermits were saints," she pointed out in mild reproach.

"Ah, yes, they triumphed! More, in spite of what Swinburne wrote, than the pale Galilean. But that needn't mean that the pale ones weren't equally valid. Indeed, I maintain that they were more so! And I suggest further, Aunt Jane, that when an attraction existed between two of them, an attraction, let us say, that could not be lawfully indulged, they would use it to intensify their Christian love so that love became a radiant flame! It may even have been so between the beloved disciple and our Lord. St. John may have adored the master with all his soul, with all his heart, with all his mind, and, yes, with all his body!"

"But they were men," Jane gasped.

"There can be such affections among men, Aunt Jane. Look at the Greeks."

"Gordon!"

"Now don't get excited. I am talking about *sublimated* things." The young man's eyes now flashed with such authority that Jane felt subdued. She looked about at the stylish ladies in the booths and around at the tall brown dead walls of the gymnasium and wondered that this undeniable slice of reality could encompass so ethereal a soul as Gordon's. But *was* it ethereal? Wasn't it too fevered? Too ecstatic? He might scorn the filthy hermits of the desert sands, but did they not have expert knowledge of the devil? She closed her eyes and moved her lips in prayer.

"Aune Jane! Are you praying for me?"

"No, dear boy. For myself. I am praying that you will accept the offer I am about to make to you."

"Accept? You mean it's a present?"

"A kind of present."

"Dear Aunt Jane! Of course I accept. What is it?"

"A trip to the Holy Land. Oh, more than that. A year in the Holy Land! If you could take a leave of absence from the church."

Gordon stared at her, his eyes full of surprise and questions. "I've always wanted to go to the Holy Land," he said gravely.

"I know that. And you could learn about those early Christians you admire so. Oh, my child, it could be the —" She stopped herself. "It could be the making of you." She had almost said the "saving."

"But how could I accept such a gift? And how could you afford it?"

"I have my savings."

"Your savings? Oh, Aunt Jane, how could I take *them*?"

"To make me happy. And to please God. I believe he wishes you to go."

Again he stared at her, and she seemed to make out a tiny diamond glittering in each pupil. He was so intense that he had to moisten his lips before he spoke. "You mean you've had guidance?"

"Yes!" she cried recklessly. "Guidance!" She clasped her hands. "Oh, my boy, I *know* you must go!"

He looked down for a long time at the floor in silent study. "I suppose a true friend would understand if God really meant me to go."

"A true friend?" She was afraid that she might have exposed herself by the very rigidity of her failure to glance in the direction of a certain booth.

"A friend who really loved me would have to appreciate the necessity of my going," he continued pensively.

"Like those early Christians."

He looked up suspiciously. "Aunt Jane, you're not laughing at me?"

"Never, dear boy. Not for all the world!"

"But of course you can accept them, Jane! He took them expressly for you!"

She was standing with her brother John in her dining room, on whose cleared table she had laid out the photographs of the fourteen stations of the cross that Gordon had sent her from Jerusalem.

"But they're so beautiful, John. They should be hung in the parish house."

"Well, of course, they're yours to give to anyone you want. But I think Mr. Muir would like you to keep them. After all, if you were inspired to send him on that trip, couldn't he have been inspired to take these pictures for you?"

Was John smiling at her? She turned back to the pictures, so eerily moving in their blacks and pale whites. They showed the simplest of street scenes, empty of people: a doorway, an archway, a bit of wall, cobblestones, an ogee against the sky, a sidewalk, glassless gaping holes for windows. Why were they so powerful? She recalled the moving passage of Gordon's letter:

> I walked every day in the steps of our Lord until I could almost imagine that I felt the weight of the cross on my shoulders and the prick of the thorns on my brow. I wanted to give you something of that wonderful experience.

And Jane indeed felt he had succeeded when the pictures had been framed and hung by the stairs from the hall to the third floor. She made it a habit, when she came down for breakfast, to pause each morning before a different station and say a prayer.

The prayer was said for Gordon. She made her little daily plea to the Almighty that he would meet and marry a fine young woman who would be worthy of him. She was beginning to dare to hope that the trip to Jerusalem was accomplishing its real purpose and that her pilgrim would return cured of his insane infatuation, and hope waxed stronger on the afternoon when her brother John called to give her the great news that the Bullocks were to be transferred to a parish in Georgia.

"It will be a great loss to us all, of course," he said, "but Mr. Bullock himself requested the transfer. He believes he has been stationed long enough in a rich community. He feels he must work now with the poor. I must confess, I find that an admirable sentiment."

"But poor Mrs. Bullock, won't she miss New York?"

"I don't suppose so. You know, she's from the South."

"I must call on her right away."

"You won't find her. Mr. Bullock told me she's gone south to make things ready in their new house."

Jane now began to wonder if she had not been wrong from the beginning. And was it possible that the small flat feeling in her heart was disappointment? Shame on you, Jane Lyle! The next morning she paused before two stations of the cross and said two prayers. One was for Gordon's future bride. The other was to beg forgiveness for herself, a suspicious, meddling old fool.

She found she had favorites among the stations. The

seventh, where Jesus stumbled for the second time, particularly held her attention. Under the glazed white of a dead sky, the large rusticated stones that framed an arched doorway leading into blackness stood out so sharply that she seemed to touch their coarseness, feel their dankness. As in the other thirteen there was no living creature to be seen, not even an ass or a dove, and it was as if no living thing could have existed there. Yet there nonetheless emanated from the simple scene an aura of intense emotion; Jane felt her heart quicken. Did it come from the blackness that filled the archway? What was that darkness? What was in it or behind it? Although it seemed to throb with power, it did not inspire fear but simply awe. The stones on the street and in the walls gave out a thick sweet essence. Gordon must have been right. Jesus had passed there, stumbled there. Jesus was still there.

Jane would now feel a weight in her heart that was not entirely unpleasurable when she was walking in the neighborhood and happened to think of the prints. She had always considered the brownstone façades with their curtained windows as stern, rather formidable walls whose function was to keep out all but the very distinctly invited. But now these exteriors, as if responding to her vision of the streets in Jerusalem, seemed russet rather than chocolate, and the slant of afternoon light across the panes of their windows gave her spirits an almost joyous lift.

Yet these sensations did not make her feel altogether easy. What had a redoubtable Scotch Presbyterian old maid to do with this softening of the fibers, this faster pacing of the blood, this desire to smile benignly at total strangers? What had such lightness of heart to do with the anguished tread of our Lord through those grim alleyways?

Nor was she at all reassured by the long letter that she received from Gordon in answer to hers about her mixed reactions to his pictures.

I am so happy, dearest Aunt Jane, at what you tell me about the force of your response. It is true that the prints are pregnant with emotion; feeling seems to seep out of the very walls my camera has reproduced, like the moisture that dampens your hands when you touch them. And what could that feeling be, in its true essence, but love, the love in which the sacred streets are saturated, the love for us of our mortal God as he was about to yield up his mortality? It is a love that encompasses everyone, even the Roman centurions and the Jews who scourged him and crowned him with thorns, even the people in the streets who spat at him and reviled him as he passed along, dragging his cross. Yes, all are included in that abounding emotion, as all are included in that abounding pain. What you see in my pictures is most certainly there: the ineffable, the exquisite union of love and sorrow, the marriage of ecstasy and agony.

Jane read this letter over many times with a slowly gathering doubt that seemed to materialize at last into a very dark cloud. It was a cloud over the too new, or too garish sky of what she suddenly and fiercely denounced as her emotional "romp." Standing before her once favorite of the stations, she fancied that she could now sense something very different in the darkness of the doorway, something grinning and fetid, something redolent of the dirty bazaars of the Middle East, something covetous and cheating and mean. And then, as she closed her eyes with a sudden sick despair, she seemed to hear the clash of cymbals and pictured the writhing of sensuous shapes and the gleam of the dark eyes of cruelty and lust and the flash of scimitars that mutilated human flesh.

"Oh, my God," she moaned, "what have I done?"

A month later John Lyle stood again with his sister in her dining room as she piled on the bare table the photographs that she had taken down from the stairwell wall.

"What are you going to do with them?"

"I'll give them to the parish house."

"I don't suppose the poor pictures are to blame for what happened."

"It's not that, John," she said with a weary patience. "I just don't want them around, that's all."

"Because they remind you of him?"

"I don't need to be reminded. I shan't forget him."

"I don't imagine many of us will. I guess it's the worst scandal in the history of our church."

"Don't forget it was she who ran after him to Jerusalem!"

"But he didn't have to follow her to Paris. I'm afraid he's a very wicked young man."

"Oh, John, don't be a stuffy idiot!" she cried in an explosion of impatience. "What have you known in your easy life of his temptations? What have you known of passion?"

"Passion? You ask me that, Jane?" He looked appalled. "What have *you* known of passion, I'd like to know?"

"Oh, a bit," she said grimly, turning back to the pictures. "I may have learned it late in life, but I've learned it. I've felt it."

"My dear Jane, what can you be talking about? Has some dirty old codger had the gall to —?"

"Oh, no, no, nothing so ludicrous," she retorted with a hard, dry laugh. "Maybe I've learned it from these."

"From the stations of the cross?" He still gaped. "But, my dear sister, the passion of our Lord wasn't *that* kind of passion!"

"Wasn't it? Isn't passion passion?"

But when she looked up to see the stricken expression on his innocent, clear, wrinkled old face, she relented. There was no point smashing anything more than had already been smashed. If their brownstone walls were made of cardboard, at least they were still standing.

"No, John, I'm not crazy. You needn't call a doctor. It's just that I'm . . . well, you know what there's no fool like."

And cutting a piece of string from the spool on the table she started tying up the framed pictures in bundles of three.

The Wedding
Guest

IN THE EARLY SPRING of the first year of this century Griswold Norrie, a handsome, lean, blond young
man, whose broad shoulders and tall straight build moved
supply to his long stride, passed up Fifth Avenue at midday
towards his destination at Sixty-fifth Street, the Patroons
Club. He had come from a final fitting for the cutaway that
he would wear at his wedding to Ione Carruthers in only
four weeks' time. The sky was a glorious, cloudless light
blue, the air velvet, and his heart sparkled like the pavement
under the noon sun.

Griswold had always loved Fifth Avenue and its double
row of mansions, turning to one at Fifty-ninth Street, where
the green park began its function of supplying a view to
the more northerly proprietors. He knew all the houses
by the names of their owners and kept a mental list of those
in which he dined. But his particular interest lay in putting
together the houses constructed by his relatives, assembling
in a secret fantasy a real estate package that showed most
of the glittering avenue controlled by his kin. Here, for
example, was the high-dormered, red brick Louis XIII

château of his aunt Eleanor Frost, and two blocks north the Doric marble façade of his aunt Julia Post, and beyond that the bleak Romanesque stone box of his step-grandmother Norrie. And when he added the many great structures of the Carruthers family and the huge brownstone cube of his fiancée's late great-grandfather (unfortunately now a jewelry store), did his fantasy not approach reality? He and Ione between them would be connected by blood or marriage to every family that counted in Manhattan society!

Griswold was taking the day off from the Standard Trust Company, where he worked on the family accounts. He did not like to ask for special privileges — he had every intention, despite his personal means, of being a serious banker — but there was no question that his commitments, as a junior trustee of the Patroons Club and treasurer of the Bellevue Racing Association, as a founder of the Bachelors Ball and Secretary of the Harvard Class of '91, had on occasion to take priority over the daily grind. Did not even his bosses say so? And if being seen as an active member of respected institutions had its importance in the career of a junior trust officer, how much more was his marriage into the family of the largest holder of railroad securities in the nation?

Of course, his was a marriage of love. He paused now to gaze appreciatively at the lovely nude lady washing herself high over the basin in Grand Army Plaza. Soon his bride would be displaying her own lovely limbs and body to his enraptured eye. Oh, yes, he had been to Paris; he had seen the world; he did not have to blush at such thoughts. Indeed, Ione and he had come close to a frank discussion of future intimacies — for Ione regarded herself as a modern woman — or at least as close as he had allowed her. At a certain point he deemed it prudent to pull her up. She had a way of pushing ahead into realms where women should tread with reserve. She was too fond, for example, of reading Veblen and was always pointing out egregious examples of his or her family's "conspicuous consumption." But after one of her flights of fancy, when he would summon her back to reality with a gentle "Where is my giddy angel soaring to?" she would fling her arms about his neck and kiss him warmly on the lips and cry: "Don't worry, sweetheart, I'll always come home to strong sensible *you!*"

Entering the Patroons Club he paused to take in the splendor of its marble hall with the vaulted Adamesque ceiling and the Palladian archway leading to the monumental red-carpeted stairway. As his father put it: "Stanford White is the only architect who can build for gentlemen." But Lewis Norrie, who was as cynical as he was conservative, and as intelligent as he was hard-headed, would then go on to add: "The Patroons is the last men's club that won't even permit an annual ladies' day. But I wonder if you, my boy, at the rate we're going, won't live to see it go down like Custer's Last Stand!"

Griswold thought of this now, for it was not unrelated to the topic he had come to discuss with his father. The latter put down his newspaper as his son approached him in the reading room, and the two of them silently repaired to the dark, glinting, cavernous bar where the senior drank iced gin and the junior, considering the early hour, a glass of fizzy water.

"I want Atalanta to come to my wedding," Griswold began boldly. "I want you to speak to Mrs. Carruthers about it. It's unthinkable that my grandfather's widow should not be present on the occasion."

Mr. Norrie pursed his lips and coughed. He was not taken by surprise; these signals were simply to underscore the acknowledged gravity of the subject. He was a gentleman of sixty who seemed to be made out of highly durable leather. The gray hair looked as hard as a statue's, and the serene eyes seemed not so much cold as all-seeing. Griswold inwardly charged his father with living in a very small world — he prided himself that his own was much less limited — but he recognized that the old boy knew every nook and cranny of that restricted domain.

"I think you might leave that issue to me, Grissy." There was only the faintest reproach in the clear flat tone. "After all, if she is the widow of your grandfather, she is the widow of my father. That, it seems to me, should give me the prior responsibility."

Griswold knew that his father would never refer to the lady as his "stepmother." It was not only that Atalanta was the same age as his father; she had married old Mr. Norrie over the violent opposition of the entire family. Cyrus Norrie, the founder of the fortune, had been over seventy at his second wedding and approaching senility. Atalanta Ferris had been — well, almost everything, a female preacher, a suffragette, a medium, an advocate of companionate marriage and free love. She had become famous in the seventies, shaking her long red locks on platforms, inciting audiences to near riot in this cause or that, a handsome demagogue, a maenad. Old Mr. Norrie had consulted her about investments and had been impressed by her divinations. He had defied his son and daughters in making her his wife and further defied them in leaving her a third of his huge oil-derived fortune. After years of bitter litigation this had been reduced to a fifth, but even this had been considered "highway robbery" by Griswold's aunts.

"But, Father, leaving it to you would mean she'd never be invited. And as you know, I have been seeing her. We have become friends. I feel she has been misjudged by my aunts. And I feel very strongly, as the only son of Grandpa's only son, that I should take a stand in favor of her more decent treatment."

His father nodded, as if to do this proposition justice. Hardly ever in his life had Griswold seen him lose his temper, and then only in minor matters of maintenance where servants had not done as they had been instructed. "I call on Atalanta every New Year's Day," he observed. "All the people at her reception can see me do it. Of course, your mother does not come, and I thought it wiser not to urge her. I also see Atalanta occasionally on matters of family business. There is no acrimony between us, for I do not share the violent feelings of your aunts. I think I understand Atalanta better than they do. But the real point, Grissy, is this. Atalanta is just as willing as I am to leave things as they are. She respects me, I believe, without in the least liking me. I feel the same way about her. Why can't you accept a modus vivendi that she and I have worked out and that is satisfactory to both?"

"Because, sir, if you will forgive me, I cannot believe that it is, at least to her. I believe that Atalanta considers herself deeply wronged by my aunts and by Mother. I believe she has welcomed my visits and my offer of friendship. I consider her a remarkable woman. I want to show before all the world that I take my grandfather's wife by the hand."

"You'll reap the whirlwind, my son," Lewis Norrie muttered with a grunt. "You don't know the power you will be challenging. If you ask Atalanta to your wedding you may have nobody else there. Including your bride!"

"Oh, Ione is with me on this!" Griswold exclaimed. "Ione feels just as I do."

"Has she talked to her mother?"

"Not yet. That's why we decided to appeal to you. We thought Mrs. Carruthers would be more apt to come around if you spoke to her."

"Oh, so *I* am chosen to walk into the dragon's lair? Thank you very much, but I think I shall leave the pleasure of that particular form of suicide to those who propose it. I am delighted, dear boy, at the prospect of your union with the enchanting and amiable Ione, but I do not consider it one of the duties of her prospective father-in-law to take on the formidable Elsa."

"Oh, Father, come, Mrs. Carruthers isn't that bad."

"My dear son, you're simply talking through your hat. I can see that chapeau in front of your mouth just as clearly as if you hadn't checked it in the cloakroom. Elsa Carruthers has been sweet-mouthing you because you're one of the most eligible bachelors in New York. No, don't frown and shrug your shoulders: you *are*, my boy. Have you ever stopped to consider how mothers like Elsa dread the sleazy fortune hunters who inhabit this town? And then along comes Griswold Norrie, clean, intelligent, without vices or degrading attachments, handsome to behold and damn near as rich as her daughter. By God, of course she has to have you! But even so, don't kid yourself. Once she has you, or once you cross her on a real issue, that sweet smile will vanish, and the true Elsa will spring like the armed Athena from the brain of Zeus!"

"And will poor Atalanta really present such an issue?"

" 'Poor' Atalanta! How your aunts wish she were that. But certainly, she would present it. The women of your mother's and Elsa's world can never forgive her her past. According to them, she's no better than a prostitute."

"Father! You surely don't believe she was that."

"I don't know what she was, my boy. I admit I find it hard to believe that she ever sold herself. However, it seems indisputable that she had love affairs. After all, she advocated free unions."

"But not after she married Grandpa?"

"So far as I know she has been utterly respectable ever since she married your grandfather."

"Well, why should we care what happened before? If *he* didn't?"

"Of course, we don't know that he knew. He was not the man he had been when he married her. But who are 'we'? The men? What do we count for? The women are down on her, no matter how pure she was after her marriage. And do you know why? Because a woman who gives her body to a man without making a husband of him is considered a traitor to her sex. The only way they can cope with our power is through marriage. And a woman who is unchaste is exposing her sex to the enemy!"

Griswold sighed. He knew that when his father took refuge in theorizing it was to avoid the principal issue. And when he avoided that it was because he had decided not to grant what had been requested. And his mind, once made up, was unchangeable.

"I see that I shall have to speak to Mrs. Carruthers myself. Do you think I might use the French analogy? She's very keen on things European."

"What do you mean by the French analogy?"

"In France a fallen woman may be ostracized by society but never by the family."

"Elsa would point out that your wedding is going to be attended by several hundred people who are not family."

"But we could *have* it just family."

"With a million dollars' worth of wedding presents already received? Isn't that the figure the tabloids are quoting? If you think Elsa Carruthers is going to marry her daughter in some kind of hugger-mugger ceremony, you are dreaming."

Griswold rose. "All I can do anyway is try."

His father merely cackled.

Griswold knew that his father was not exaggerating the formidable aspect of his mother-in-law-to-be. Priding himself on the cosmopolitan education that he had received on his "grand tour" — a whole year of London, Paris and Rome — he thought he could classify Mrs. Carruthers as a uniquely American type: the plain, stocky woman who, without any great pretensions of family or fortune (her father had been Commandant of the Brooklyn Navy Yard) had managed to capture the charming son of the richest man in New York. And it had all been done, too, so far as Griswold could make out, by force of character and the simple willingness to be disagreeable at the right moment. Of course Mr. Carruthers had not been faithful to his Elsa — even she could not ask for everything — but he had taken great, if unsuccessful, pains to conceal his infidelities.

Elsa Carruthers had pale skin, flabby on the cheeks, a square chin, thin long lips, agate staring eyes and straight black-olive hair. She spent large sums on dress and on big jewelry, yet she wore it all carelessly, as if aware of not needing it for her real purpose, which was simply to dominate. Griswold, who liked to think he had an eye for a setting, would have dressed her in black, with a white collar, against a decor of dark sinister French Renaissance — a Catherine de' Medici — but she insisted instead on a totally inappropriate Louis XV background in vast chambers full of panels showing ladies in swings with lovers peeping.

Today he found her and Ione in the library where the presents were arranged on long trestle tables guarded by a detective. He might have imagined himself on the main floor of Tiffany's. Ione, as radiant as one of the painted ladies in a swing, as fresh and dark-eyed as one of the Nattier portraits, managing to seem docile and obedient to her mother while at the same time conveying the idea that she could assert herself whenever she needed to, listened gravely as her betrothed explained his bizarre purpose to her parent.

"But my precious Grissy," Mrs. Carruthers at last exclaimed with a dry, brittle laugh, "you must know that what you are proposing is quite out of the question. I suppose you are speaking, as the lawyers say, for the record. Very well, let us accept it as that and consider the matter closed. You are perfectly free to place the blame entirely on my shoulders. Tell Mrs. Norrie that you pleaded unsuccessfully for her invitation. She will understand." She turned now to the table nearest her. "Will you look at this magnificent parure from Ione's Aunt Natalie that has just arrived. Have you ever seen such rubies?"

Ione took the necklace from the black box and held it to her throat as she whirled around her fiancé in a waltz.

"Look, Gris! You're marrying a princess!"

Griswold drew himself up, refusing to be distracted. "Please, Mrs. Carruthers! Please, Ione! I must discuss this. It means so much to me."

He had a distinct sense that Ione was lost to the cause.

The moment her mother had raised the flag of unity, she had bowed. The two ladies listened with unconcealed impatience while he again stated his case, in tedious detail. He was making no headway.

"Look, Griswold," Elsa Carruthers stated at last in her firmest tone, which was very firm, "even if I were disposed to oblige you as a happy addition to my family, even if I sincerely wanted to do this favor for you, I could not. My position in society would forbid it. You men of the Patroons Club may not take New York society seriously, but thousands of others do. Society is not just a question of dressing up and giving parties. It is a question of setting a moral example for the whole community. If a woman like Mrs. Norrie came to this house at my invitation and was introduced under my aegis to my friends, the inference would be clear that I approve of her moral character. That I approve of unchastity and free love! And that I cannot allow!" Elsa seemed carried away by the force of her own rhetoric. She actually stamped her foot. "No, Griswold Norrie, that you cannot ask of me. Never, never, never!"

He caught the flash of alarm in Ione's eyes as she stepped over to place a warning hand on his arm. "Please, darling," she murmured. "It's not good for Mamma to get so excited. Remember her heart."

"Very well, I shall not ask you to invite her," he retorted in choked tones. "I shall invite her myself. I shall ask her to come as the guest of the groom. Surely it is proper to accord the groom and his family a list of invitees. I shall limit mine to Mrs. Atalanta Norrie."

"And do you know what I shall do if that woman dares to cross my threshold, *Mister* Griswold Norrie?" Elsa's eyes were now bulging, and her voice rose almost to a shout. "Did you see *Lady Windermere's Fan?* Well, I shall do what Lady Windermere only threatened to do. I shall strike that woman across her face with my fan!"

Ione hurried over to her mother, put an arm protectively around her shoulders and led her from the room. She was gone for fifteen minutes. When she returned alone she was very cool and poised.

"I'm surprised to find you still here. Haven't you done enough for one day? Do you want to kill my mother?"

"Ione, darling, I never thought —"

"You never thought, I know. But think now, Griswold. You cannot possibly expect Mrs. Norrie to come here to be insulted, nor can you risk Mother's heart by allowing her to insult her. Give up your foolish idea. Would you like me to go to Mrs. Norrie and explain the whole thing?"

"But that's my job!"

"As I've said already, don't you think you've done enough? This is women's work, my dear. You had far better stay out of it altogether."

Griswold felt his heart pounding in sudden violent gratitude at what this enchanting creature was willing to do for him. He stepped forward to clasp her in his arms and was deeply relieved that she did not repulse him.

"My angel, you're right. Of course you're right. How could you not be? I'll take you to call on Atalanta, but not till I've explained to her first how things are."

Atalanta Norrie continued to occupy her late husband's gray stone tomb of a mansion on Fifth Avenue and Fifty-seventh Street. It seemed to have no function but to repel;

it was devoid of decoration except for its Romanesque windows, and its interior was made up of huge, sparsely furnished, needlessly dark chambers. Its owner did not entertain, but she was surrounded by a motley court of hangers-on, some of whom seemed to live in the upper stories — muttering ancient women, presumably relations, and young, colorfully dressed, apparently unemployed young men. It was widely believed that Mrs. Norrie gave lessons in spiritualism to her disciples.

She received her step-grandson alone. The tall, exotic, red-haired female preacher had filled out into a strong, straight, rather massive woman of sixty, with a firm, almost unlined face and thick gray hair piled in layers, like a pagoda, over her high brow. The eyes, large and expressionless, were fixed on Griswold as he made his stumbling explanation.

"I understand everyone's position with the utmost clarity," Atalanta said at last. "I am not in the least interested in going to Mrs. Carruthers's against her will. I shall go to the church to see you married, dear boy, and that will be quite enough for me. I don't suppose that Elsa Carruthers will deny me a seat in the house of God, even *her* God. The only reason that I allowed you to requst an invitation for me to the reception was to see if you could stand up to them."

"Them? Don't you mean her?"

"Certainly not. I mean her *and* her daughter. I mean the women. The women of your world."

"They're very fine women," Griswold insisted.

"Fine is not an exact term. They know they're engaged in a war, and you don't."

"Oh, a war, Atalanta, really!"

"Really," she echoed him grimly. "Because you and I have become friends, I decided to help you. To rescue you, before it was too late. Listen to me, Griswold. Put your prejudices in the corner for a minute and listen to me. Don't worry. I'll give them back to you. Almost intact." Atalanta paused now as if to decide how best to proceed. Then she nodded. "Let us start with your grandmother. My predecessor. I have learned what I could about her. She was like all the wives of the financial pioneers. Simple, religious, awed by her dominating husband, awkward in society, nostalgic for the day when she did the sewing and helped the maid-of-all-work. She learned not to wince when her more sophisticated children found her gauche. She consoled herself in church work. But her hidden resentment was passed on to her daughters and daughters-in-law. *They* were determined that her fate would not be theirs. Their tool would be society. With palaces and parties, they would shackle the weaker sons and grandsons of the tycoons. In golden chains! And how they've done it! Look at your father. Look at Ione's uncles. The wife's revenge was castration!"

"Atalanta!" Griswold jumped to his feet in horror.

"I wanted to save you," she continued imperturbably. "But now I am very much afraid it's too late. I can only look into the future and see what I can see. Sit down again, dear boy, and hold my hand."

Griswold sat beside her and held that large cold hand in both of his. Atalanta closed her eyes and was silent for two minutes. It seemed much longer. When she spoke, her eyes still closed, it was in a slow monotone.

"Let the years pass. Many years. I see you in an office. You will not have to work, but it will get you out of the house, which will be Ione's domain. I see you lunching with your friends and planning fishing and hunting trips. I do not see you indulging in furtive adulteries."

"Thanks," he breathed.

"But at times you may regret your fidelity."

"Please, Atalanta!"

"Hush!" She opened her eyes to look at him blankly and closed them again. "Ah, yes, *now* I see. You are sitting in a club in the late afternoon, having come there from the office — you come there every afternoon. You are tired, and you hope you can dine there with old friends over gin and fishing stories. You hope it is not a night when your wife is entertaining. Then the butler always calls the club at six to tell you to be home in time to dress, and you know when this has happened because you see a page crossing the floor towards you carrying a small silver tray with a message. Oh, yes, you are weary. You are praying this night will be a free one and that you can relax behind the high walls of your sanctuary. You think the dread moment is safely past and you are raising the ice-cold gin to your thirsty lips . . . oh, what heaven! . . . But no, now you observe the spot of red in the big doorway, and it grows before your tired eyes into the form of the page, and you see that he is carrying a small silver tray, and yes —"

"Atalanta! I'm leaving!"

He and Ione stood in the library before the long trestle tables with the presents. He was very grave, but she was smiling, a bit oddly.

"*Say* it, Gris, darling! Say what's on your mind."

"If I can't have my grandfather's widow at my wedding reception, I don't want anybody there!"

She nodded, considering it. "I can see that. Yes, I think I can see that."

"Would you marry me without a wedding reception? Now? Or next week?" He could hardly believe it when she did not scream. "Oh, darling, *would* you?"

"That's what you really and truly want?"

"Yes!"

"And you really and truly believe it's for our greater happiness?"

"Oh, I do!"

"Then I agree."

"Angel!" He swept her into his arms, wondering wildly if it wasn't dangerous to be so happy. Then his eye took in the rows of presents over her shoulder. "Look at all this crazy gold and silver! Doesn't it seem to be laughing at us?"

She disengaged herself from his embrace. "These things, of course, must all be sent back."

"What do you mean?"

"If we cancelled the reception and kept the presents, we'd be guilty of a fraud. People expect something for what they've spent."

Griswold, stunned, began to move slowly along one of the tables. "Good heavens, what a job!" He picked up a silver epergne and put it down. He leaned over a magnificent George II tray. A horrible thought struck him. "But, Ione, all this stuff is monogrammed with our initials."

"It does make it awkward, I admit. But it can hardly alter the principle."

Griswold now began feverishly to examine the different objects. A complete set of the finest damask table linen from his aunt Eleanor Frost, with the huge woven letters *G* and *I* interlaced over an *N*. A set of gold service plates from his aunt Julia Post similarly dedicated; a vast diamond clip pin from his aunt Mabel Onderdonk with the fatal initials set in sapphires. On and on — there seemed no end to it.

"We can't do it," he groaned. "We just can't do it!"

"Then we must go through with the reception."

And he knew now that he would never know whether or not she had believed, even for a minute, that they wouldn't.

Marcus:
A Gothic Tale

MARCUS SUMNER had been one of the first students at Clare when the school had opened, a circle of Tudor gray on a verdant tract of land near Fitchburg, Massachusetts, in the autumn of 1905. The young founding headmaster, the Reverend Philemon Forrester, had inspired the confidence of Marcus's banking father, who, like all of his peers in Manhattan, holding to the creed that male progeny could be educated only in New England, had sent his ailing and precocious motherless child to be placed under the special care of the principal and his wife. Marcus, happy to be removed from the tutelage of his stern, elderly sire, and protected from the roughness of schoolmates by the headmaster, in whose house he actually lived, had sunk deep roots in the Forrester family and had grown up as a kind of adoring eldest son or younger brother of Philemon. When he graduated from Clare he spent only the necessary four years at Harvard before returning to the expanded school to become its youngest faculty member and to dedicate his life and the fortune that he had now inherited from his deceased parent to the glory of Clare and Philemon Forrester.

The latter was a huge man with a great square blocky head and long, prematurely gray locks that suggested the cleric of an earlier era. He was so moving a preacher that many deplored his isolation in a private school, and there were always those ready to propose him for a bishopric. But Forrester seemed contented in that smaller sphere, which he dominated so absolutely. The souls of four hundred boys were enough for him, plus the parishioners of neighboring churches in which he regularly preached, and the readers of his published sermons and spiritual poems. He was happy to labor in his own vineyard, regarding his oratorical gift as an endowment from God for that purpose. And was he really good enough even for that? There were moments when, standing in the pulpit before commencing an address, the eyes under those bushy eyebrows tightly closed in silent orison, he seemed to be clutching for an inspiration that might at any time be withdrawn.

Marcus Sumner, on the other hand, small, spindly and pale, with thick blond hair and green burning eyes, deprived by a fibrillating heart of all sports but sailing, and that only with a crew for the heavy work, found in the mansion of the headmaster's soul enough rooms for all the love of which he deemed his nature capable. What return, what contribution could he make to such a man, who was all the deity he needed, even in the craggy Gothic school chapel? What service could he render to a god who worshiped God? But Marcus was not long in concluding that if the juggler of Anatole France's tale could bring his tricks to the altar, so could he offer his scholarship as an embellishment of the school. And Forrester, having first dutifully warned the young man that he ought to see something more of the world before shutting himself up in a New England boarding school, having reminded him that Clare and its headmaster already occupied too large a space on his horizon, had given in before Marcus's stricken look. Perhaps he recognized that a rejection might prove fatal, and had therefore accepted a responsibility not to be escaped. He embraced the trembling slim shoulders with these warm words:

"Very well, dear boy, come to us, come to us, by all means. We shall profit by your fine appreciation of letters and be heartened by your faith in our undertakings. And it need not be forever. We can always release you when occasion beckons. Oh, yes, we can even push you up the ladder of fame!"

"When I leave Clare," Marcus cried in the passion of his gratitude, "it will be feet first!"

In the classroom Marcus would confront his pupils without a textbook. He would make no reference to the given assignment for the day. Pulling up the old map of the Roman Empire that covered his blackboard he would reveal the sonnet or short poem or quotation that he had chalked thereon, without indication of date or author. He would then, for the given hour, limit the discussion to the phrases and words before the eyes of the class, reciting the lines one by one in different tones, from the mocking to the sublime, revealing feelingly towards the end of the period, his own emotions, either for or against the poem, and calling for assent or dissent. At first he encountered sullen silence, then ridicule and at last applause. Little by little Mr. Sumner became "the thing." Some boys actually began to read poetry without its being assigned. Others became enthusiasts. A few even caught fire.

The most brightly burning of these, Rodman Venable,

was a dark, handsome boy, tall and very thin, with enormous brooding eyes, who would stare at Marcus as if he could not believe that the latter could really mean anything as daring and original as he seemed to be saying, which made the disconcerted teacher search his mind to see if he could not come up with something that would not let the boy down. Rodman became a quick, too quick convert to the doctrine of Walter Pater; he wanted to burn with a hard, gemlike flame, and it was he who suggested to Marcus that he invite a select group of students to spend a part of their summer vacation with him.

"I understand, sir, that you have a shingle palace on Long Island Sound and a trim sailing yacht. We could recite Keats and Shelley as we buffeted the waves of the wine-dark sea! Aren't such vacation visits common between masters and boys in the English public schools?"

Well, of course they were, and Marcus was enchanted with the idea. The month of July was chosen, and the visitors, all poetry enthusiasts, were selected by Rodman. He hilariously compared the project to that in *Love's Labour's Lost* where the king and peers agree to abjure the company of women in favor of study. They would sail in the morning, read in the afternoon and engage in Platonic dialogues at night.

When Marcus told the headmaster of his plan, however, the latter showed a decidedly guarded enthusiasm, and the very next weekend Marcus was asked to meet Rodman's father in Mr. Forrester's study, vacated by the headmaster for the occasion.

Mr. Venable was a species of gentleman with whom Marcus was not familiar: the New Yorker who emulated the cultural aspirations of Boston. He sat in his armchair with an artful combination of stiffness and ease, as if he were a visiting legate to whom the proconsul had had temporarily to yield his bench of authority. He was serene, bald, glacial, and absolutely still, except for a finger that stroked the full, silky mustache.

"I do not for a minute, Mr. Sumner, wish to convey any disapproval of your inspiring my boy to a love of fine poetry. Yours is a noble calling and one, if I may say so between ourselves, that fills a definite need at Clare. Mr. Forrester, for all his undoubted virtues and vibrant faith, is hardly an intellectual man."

Marcus clenched his fists in a sudden spasm of uncontrollable resentment. "Oh, sir! How can you say that?"

Mr. Venable's bland, tan eyes widened slightly. "My dear Mr. Sumner, his verse! Surely you, of all men, are not going to defend 'Oh, Jesus, have I hurt you? Your pain lies at my door'?"

Marcus's heart seemed to be rolling about under his rib cage. He had so successfully suppressed all awareness of the headmaster's revivalist hymns that any reminder of them came as a whiplash across the cheek. "We might say that his stanzas are the crumbs of the feast of his faith," he muttered.

"Very well put, Mr. Sumner! And I value loyalty above all other qualities in a schoolmaster. But to the matter in hand. I am of the opinion that Rodman would be better at home this summer than with you. I am aware that you have a charming house on the North Shore and a beautiful sailing yacht, but I understand that the company will be entirely male and that there will be long sessions where music and art and beauty will be ardently discussed."

"And that is objectionable?"

"Surely you are not unaware, Mr. Sumner, of the excesses to which sentimentality among ardent and impressionable young men may lead?"

Marcus looked at him with horror. "To what do you refer, sir?"

"Well, you are too young, of course, to remember the Oscar Wilde business, but surely you have heard of it?"

"Mr. Venable!" Marcus leaped to his feet. "You cannot think —?"

"Oh, but I *do*, Mr. Sumner. Not that you would in any way foster such horrors, of course. I am talking only of possibilities. And with boys all things are possible. Boys can be vicious, sir! And if you don't know that, you should learn it as soon as possible."

Marcus sat down again, crumpled. "You mean such things go on here? At Clare?"

"My son has implied to me that they do."

"Not surely . . . ? I mean . . . not *he*?"

"Oh, no." Venable shook his head decisively. "But he has not manifested as much disgust at those who may have been guilty as I should like to see. He seems to have adopted what I hesitate to call a fashionable tolerance for vice and perversion. There is a kind of 'Oh, Daddy, don't be provincial' sneer in his attitude that I find most disturbing. That is why I think he will do better this summer with his family in Narragansett where there will be golf and tennis and young ladies and dances. We can safely leave Keats and Shelley until the fall."

"And Oscar Wilde."

Venable's eyes at this showed a hint of concern that he might have gone too far. He contemplated the devastated creature before him with something like dismay. "You mustn't take these things too hard, Mr. Sumner. Perhaps you will come in July and visit us for a week. I think Rodman would like that."

"I'm afraid I must stay on Long Island. I have asked the other boys. Though perhaps that should be canceled now."

"My dear Mr. Sumner, you are going much too far!"

"How can I?" cried Marcus as he hurried from the room.

Late that night, after the boys in his dormitory had gone to bed, the headmaster himself knocked at Marcus's study door.

"Venable said he had upset you. May we discuss it?" Taking in now the younger man's emotional state, Forrester closed the door leading to the dormitory. Then he put his arm around Marcus's shoulders and allowed him to sob. "You take it too hard, my boy. Venable accused you of nothing."

"Except of living in a fool's paradise!"

"Well, that may be a very sensible place to live."

Marcus broke away from his senior. "Does that mean you think I *do*, sir?"

"No, no, of course not. Calm yourself."

"How can I? If that kind of thing goes on here among the boys!"

"Oh, did he say that?"

"He said that Rodman had implied it. And that Rodman tolerated it, too."

Forrester pursed his lips as if he were about to whistle. Then he turned and paced the length of the little chamber and back, swinging his arms slowly, pondering something. "Tell me, Marcus. If Venable were your father, might you not find him a difficult parent to love?"

"I'm afraid I should find him difficult not to hate."

"And do you not suppose that Rodman may also experience some of that difficulty?"

"Perhaps."

"And if Rodman disliked his father, would it not be natural for him to wish to hurt him?"

"I suppose so."

"And how better could he do that than by instilling in the paternal mind the suspicion that his son had had at least a taste of vicious activities?"

"But that would be at his own expense, sir!"

"I wonder, Marcus, if you have any conception of how far a child will go to revenge himself upon a parent."

Marcus quailed before the worldly wisdom of his god. Then he closed his eyes as he made himself consider the grievous problems that faced a headmaster. And he, puny ridiculous Marcus, dared to question the warrior in the front row of so savage a battle!

"I resign my post, sir. I am unworthy of it."

"Now, now, my boy, we'll sleep on this. Things will take their proper shape in the light of morning. You have been hurt. That is regrettable, but in the long run the experience may be of value. It will toughen you. Go to bed now. And remember: Clare needs you. And I am happy to think that you need Clare."

Marcus, however, did not sleep that night. Through the long hours the features of Rodman Venable bobbed up and down in his fevered brain. The dark eyes had become yellow, leering. He was like the young Apollo of the medieval legends of the survival of pagan gods into the Christian era, disguised, proscribed, but still possessed of magical powers, inciting the youths with his charm and flute and dancing feet to the pursuit of strange pleasures, unspeakable joys, until in their frenzy they would tear him to pieces. Rodman's ears began to seem pointed; now he was Pan, capable of killing as well as loving. Now he was nude and beckoning with a lewd smile that seemed to mock Marcus's reluctance. And Marcus, leaping from his bed and hurrying to the window to look up at the stars and pray, saw Rodman's laughing eyes in the pale horror of the morn. Yes, he wanted to do those things, whatever they were; he wanted to do them with Pan!

The next day Marcus resigned his position at Clare. Forrester pleaded with him for a day and most of a night, but he was adamant. He finished the term, to give the school time to find his replacement, and never again addressed a single word in private to Rodman Venable. When he was free at last, he closed his house on the North Shore and sailed for France. He took rooms at the Crillon in Paris where he decided to remain indefinitely, adopting an unvarying solitary routine. His mornings were devoted to walks and museums; his afternoons to reading in his suite; his evenings to theatre and ballet. He had no idea of what he was going to do with the rest of his life, and he tried not to think about it.

He went four times to see *Phèdre* at the Comédie Française. It seemed to him that Racine, through Réjane, was speaking directly to him. But what was the message? He pondered every scene, every couplet of the great play. Always before he had thought of the heroine as evil because she falsely accuses her stepson of attempted rape. But now it began to seem to him that Racine was showing Phèdre as too distracted by passion and baffled by circumstance to be responsible for her acts. Her real sin is the mere existence of her passion.

But could that really be? Marcus asked himself as he wandered through the brilliant gardens of the Tuileries in the incomparable spring of 1914. Phèdre doomed to eternal fire for a merely inward feeling? Suppose she had never confessed her love, never got herself tangled up with the other characters? Suppose she had died in sole possession of her guilty secret? Would she still have been damned?

No! His very soul revolted at last from the idea. He could not believe there was sin even in the grossest lust if the lusting man shut the gates to its escape and held it tightly within. On the contrary, might not repressed emotion ferment like the juice of the grape and turn itself into fine wine? Might that not even be a way in which art was born? Might God not have put lust into the world like a vineyard to bring forth a harvest of beauty?

What was Paris itself, Paris shimmering in that glorious spring, all white and gold and light green, but an example of this? Everyone knew what revolting things went on in the French capital; they were attested to by winks and "Oo-la-la's" the world over. But was there anything more beautiful than the center of the great city, a soul much finer than the vulgar body that encased it? And in his own case, was there any reason that a certain stirring within should not be converted to a purely aesthetic sense and guide? If Oscar Wilde had carried his urgings to the depths of vice, had not Walter Pater raised them to the heights of which the poets sing?

So absorbed was Marcus in his own thoughts that the outbreak of war caught him almost by surprise. The only friend he had in Paris was an old one of his mother's, a Bostonian expatriate, Mrs. Lyman Perkins, at whose house in the Parc Monceau he paid a weekly visit at tea time. She vigorously counseled him not to "slink home," but to stay in France and do war work.

"It's going to be a long war, the wiser folk are saying."

They were seated on the little terrace by her rose garden, a setting of elegant peace that seemed to deny her fiery tone. "Don't believe this 'home by Christmas' rot. You say you have no goal in life. Why not work for civilization? The poor Belgians are pouring over the frontier. They're going to need everything: shelter, food, clothing. I propose to organize all the Americans in Paris. We can set up an office right here in this house. Oh, I'll keep you busy!"

He always thought afterwards that Mrs. Perkins had provided just the tonic he needed. She was a perfectionist; her garden had the finest roses, her drawing room the love-liest *boiseries*, her table the most succulent food. She spoke French almost too well, and knew her French history and literature in depth. Yet she remained an unreconstructed New Englander who judged herself and her fellow Amer-icans by the strict old Yankee moral standards from which she regarded her French friends as somehow exempted. She was always practical and realistic, uninterested in philo-sophical or political speculations. The here and now was good enough for her; she had little use for shadows or subtleties, even in her friendships. She seemed to believe that if insight was keen enough, intimacy was unnecessary. As to the war, she adopted the prevailing violence. The Germans were barbarians who had to be crushed, and that was that.

Marcus found the war years in Paris curiously happy ones. He worked hard enough in the organization of the refugee camps and later in hospitals to feel some relief from the sense of guilt at his own exemption from the hor-ror of the trenches. He knew, after all, that he was doing all that could be expected of one of his fragile physique, and he was content to be bossed about by his own indom-itable and indefatigable general. There were moments, particularly in the dark days of 1917 before the arrival of the American troops, when he wondered if it was possible that such concentrated carnage, month after month, year after year, could be justified by any moral goal, but then he would tell himself that it was not up to him to decide these matters and that, anyway, the more carnage, the more necessary was the work that even one as puny as himself was performing. He saw unspeakable horrors in the wards that he visited, but he was somewhat consoled by the thought that for every hideous wound there was a courageous heart, that for every act of destruction there was a brave deed of defense, that for every devil there seemed to be an angel. God had a use for every seeming ill.

Mrs. Perkins herself, erect, immaculate, always in her widow's spotless black, became Marcus's symbol of the civilization that the Hun could never beat, the image of the domination of self. One had to resist the enemy within as well as without; one had to put down fear as well as lust. The world could always be beautiful to one who would not compromise.

When Mrs. Perkins died, very suddenly, after the armistice, in the flu epidemic, Marcus, awestruck in his grief, wondered if she might not have used up the capital of her fortitude and been ready, perhaps even grateful, to succumb to an efficient and speedy killer. At least she had given him the strength to return to America. It was as if she had said, in her gruff way: "Very well now; I've shown you the way. *Live!*"

When Marcus returned to Clare, after an absence of six years, he was a very different man from the unhappy and disillusioned creature who had fled to France. His slender shape had so filled out that he was almost stocky, and much of his blond hair had disappeared from his round scalp. He moved deliberately now rather than jerkily; there was something almost magisterial in the dignity of his diminutive figure, swathed in dark brown or black. Marcus had settled upon an image that would last him for the next twenty years and the personality that would go with it.

He had no favorites now among the boys, although he held small sessions for the especially gifted. There developed a legend that he had once dismissed a class because he seemed on the verge of tears in a lecture on the death of Keats. Rodman Venable had been killed in the war, and it was widely believed that it was Marcus who, in his memory, had paid for the great west window in the chapel that showed Christ with the children. He seemed to have no life outside the school, nor did he ever spend a night away from the tiny Greek Revival villa he had built just off the campus, except for one week every summer with the Forresters in Maine.

He was satisfied that he had carried the passion for beauty, which in his case was manifested not in music or color or any of the plastic arts but in words alone, words in prose or verse, to the highest and most intense pitch possible for man, and he conceived it his simple and sole duty as a citizen of the world to try to transmit this passion to any individual in the marching regiments of youth who chose to turn aside to receive it. He did not persuade himself that there would be many of these, nor did he greatly care. He was on earth, presumably, to offer a remedy to desperate souls; perhaps they had to be desperate before they sought it. For himself, anyway, he was content that beauty had entered his blood stream to satisfy his every appetite. He did not, like Omar, have any need of a jug of wine or "thou beside me singing in the wilderness"; the book of verses underneath the bough was quite enough for him. Marcus likened himself to the young Alfred de Musset, who was reputed to have swooned away on hearing a couplet in *Phèdre*.

In 1937 there was a sixth former at the school called David Prine, a scholarship boy, ungainly, large, with glossy black hair and rather wild eyes, who was so brilliant that Marcus took him on as a single student in Greek. No one else could keep up with him. Unfortunately, the boy was prone to ask awkward questions.

One evening, as they discussed Plato, Prine brought up Jowett's change of genders in translating the *Symposium*, making some of the "he's" "she's."

"How could he justify it, sir?"

"Well, you see, David, Jowett was writing for an English nineteenth-century audience. They would not have understood that kind of attachment between two men. So he deemed it better to make it between a man and a woman."

"But that doesn't make sense, sir! You told me that Plato was talking about friendship. About 'platonic' love. Wouldn't his contemporaries have been more ready to believe in a nonphysical relationship between two men than in such a one between a man and a woman? Didn't he make it harder to understand by changing the gender?"

"Plato maintained that the highest form of love was nonphysical. A friendship — perhaps what one might call a romantic friendship — between two men was the highest of all. But there were friendships in his day between men that were not platonic. That was something that troubled Plato less than it troubled the Victorians."

"Does it trouble you, sir?"

"What do you mean, David?"

"That two men should have such a friendship?"

"Such a relationship is not part of our culture. Or admitted by our religion."

"But we admire the Greeks so, sir! *You* admire them, certainly. How can you admire a people who did things of which you disapprove?"

"We live in different times, David."

"Do we, sir?"

"And now, I think the subject had better be closed."

"Oh, Mr. Sumner! I thought you were the one man in Clare I could talk to!"

But Marcus was not touched by this appeal. Indeed, he was very much relieved that David's graduation was so near at hand. He discontinued his individual instruction of the boy and told the headmaster that he had grave misgivings about his future.

Mr. Forrester, now in his sixties but as vigorous as ever, glanced down at the little man, who was walking as rapidly as he could to keep up with him. They were on their way to morning chapel.

"But the boy's a near genius, I thought you told me, Marcus. Why won't he go far?"

"I was thinking of his morals."

"Well, he'll have problems, of course. Perhaps he will find a milieu where people like that are accepted."

Marcus put his hand on Forrester's arm to support himself after this shock. "You mean you know?"

"I don't know that there's anything to *know*. As yet. And let us devoutly hope there won't be till he's out of Clare. But a headmaster learns to recognize certain types."

"You mean you can spot something like that and not move to stamp it out?"

"Oh, my dear Marcus, what powers you ascribe to a headmaster!"

"But don't you even *want* to put it down?"

"I didn't make the world. There are things in it that it is better we should accept."

"I don't agree!"

"Didn't you learn acceptance when *you* were young?"

"What do you mean, sir?" Marcus could hardly credit his hearing.

"Don't you know what I mean, Marcus?"

Marcus stopped and let the headmaster go on to chapel where he would start the service. He stared ahead at the great craggy tower shooting up into a soft, clouded, indifferent sky, a phallus thrusting into a universe that did not care, discriminate or fear. Beauty fell about his feet in a thousand fragments as if the west window that he had commissioned had shivered and been blown all over the campus.

The next day he again resigned from Clare. He reoccupied his old house and lived there henceforth alone.

The Shells
of Horace

BEING PRESIDENT of the commuters' club car oper-
ating between Brewster and Grand Central Station
was just the kind of thankless job with which Horace
Devoe was always finding himself stuck. Because he did not
have to work and commuted only in the spring and summer
from his Palladian villa and five hundred acres of landscaped
forest and meadows in Katonah to the bare, austere office on
Vanderbilt Avenue where, with the faithful Mrs. Sprit, he
clipped his coupons and paid his taxes, it was assumed by
his year-round neighbors that he had all the time in the
world to spare. "Oh, if he wants to pretend he's working,"
he could almost hear them say, "we'll see he has something
to do!" And similarly, in town in winter, because he was
known to leave his house on Park Avenue to go only as
far as his midtown private perch and not to the competitive
reality of "downtown," he was made to pay for such
simple pleasures as the opera, the symphony or the watching of animals with expensive and time-consuming trustee-
ships in opera, symphony and zoo. Of course, he was well
enough respected, but he was also certainly used. And hav-

ing no job, how could he ever retire? The balding, poker-faced, wistful little man who stared bleakly out of his page in the current 1937 edition of *Parson's Notable New Yorkers*, always laid beside the *Social Register* on his neat, bare desk, betrayed clearly enough his age of sixty.

"My dear Horace," a voice boomed in his ear, "may I have the honor of your company? May I share your pot of coffee?"

Horace looked up helplessly. Simon Regner got on the train at Mount Kisco on the rare days when he was not driven to town in his yellow Hispano-Suiza.

"Of course, Simon, please do."

When Horace had first joined the club car, back in 1921, there had been no question of Jewish members, but with the many resignations caused by the depression, the club had become more liberal. Regner, the investment banker, a rather magnificent, if stout, gentleman with flowing gray hair, a pince-nez and velvet lapels on his black suits, had been the first Jew elected.

"You can dispense with your newspaper, Horace. I can tell you the news is all bad. I had a call from Washington while I was shaving. The price of gold is down again."

Horace had no feeling against Jews, but he had been brought up to believe that they were not desirable company, and he hesitated to assume that the older generation had been entirely wrong. But what particularly embarrassed him about Regner was the latter's habit of inviting him to his grand musical evenings, which Amelia would not even consider attending. "No, darling, you go if you like. Leave me out of it. I can't abide the man." And Regner would always accept Horace's stammering excuses in good faith, waving a hand airily and saying: "Another time, another time."

"We had the pleasure of your son Douglas last night with his charming wife," Simon continued now. "They were brought to our Wagner evening by the Hulls. Oh, what you missed, Horace! Flagstad at her most sublime! And when it was over the young Devoes stayed on, and I had a real chat with your son and heir."

"Oh? And what did that young good-for-nothing have to say for himself?" Horace adopted the bantering tone deemed proper in speaking of an adult child. Why the devil should Simon Regner be interested in Douglas Devoe?

"My dear Horace, I hope you won't mind if I talk to you candidly. I assure you I have only your boy's best interests in mind."

"That boy, as you call him, is thirty-one."

"Precisely. Isn't it time he was doing something he really wants to do?"

Horace stared. "You suggest he doesn't like being a lawyer in Curtis and Day?"

"Be honest with me, Horace. Wasn't that your doing?"

"You mean his getting the job there? Well, I suppose my being a client didn't exactly hurt. Douglas's record at law school left something to be desired. But I've never interfered since."

"Would you interfere to have him made a partner?"

"Certainly not!" Horace exclaimed indignantly. "We don't do things that way." Then he reflected that his pronoun might imply that only Jews did things that way. "I mean *I* don't," he added lamely.

But Simon seemed unrebukable. He fixed his pince-nez carefully to the thin bridge of a nose that swelled out over his nostrils, and looked glitteringly at Horace. "And do you think he'll be made a partner without your assistance? Or, frankly, Horace, even with it?"

"I haven't the least idea." Horace now found the discussion positively offensive.

"Suppose I were to tell you that your son doesn't believe he ever will be made a partner?"

Horace was trapped now. If Regner had actually received Douglas's confidence, he could not ignore it. "I suppose there are other firms," he said impatiently.

Regner shook his head. "I'm afraid your son is bored with the law. And that will be fatal to his advance in any firm. But is there any reason he should practice the law at all if he doesn't like it?"

"No reason," Horace replied coolly. "Let him get another job if he wants. And if he can."

"He tells me he'd like to be a writer. That he used to write plays when he was at Harvard. Did you not approve?"

"I didn't approve or disapprove," Horace retorted testily. "But there didn't seem to be much future in it. Don't forget that since that time he's acquired a family. Five little Devoes can't be fed on one-act plays produced by avant-garde theatre groups."

Anyone else in the club car would have dropped the subject at this. The duty of self-support in a Christian adult male, no matter what the family circumstances, was never questioned. But Regner was shameless.

"Let me tell you something, Horace, that may surprise you. I gave each of my children a million dollars when they came of age."

Horace was scandalized at such lack of reticence. "I have no wish to intrude into your family finances!"

"Of course you haven't. I'm volunteering the information. And I'm volunteering more. Each one of the five has increased that sum."

"Ah, well, but they're all —" Horace stopped in time. "No doubt your children have inherited your financial acumen. Of course, I would help Douglas if he were in trouble. I give him something on his birthday and at Christmas, and big enough to be invested, too, not spent. But as for anything remotely like what you're talking about, I'm afraid he'll have to wait till I'm gone."

"But don't you see what a premium that puts on your death? You're making him look forward to it!"

"I hardly think Douglas is that sort of person. And I suggest this discussion is leading us nowhere. I happen to have very strong principles about not spoiling young people by showering them with money."

"But you came into yours when you were young."

Really, the man was impossible! "That was because I had the misfortune to lose my father early." Misfortune! Even Horace blushed at this. Would Regner have the gall to cackle with laughter? But he didn't. "And even that hardly proved a good thing for my poor brother, as no doubt you know." The club car seemed for a moment to rattle like the dice at Monte Carlo. "Perhaps our young people are not brought up to handle money like —"

"Like ours? Yes, we Jews are more realistic with our young. We trust them, for we teach them to be trustworthy. But I miss my guess if you'd be taking much of a chance with Douglas. And you'd have the joy of making an investment in his happiness. Don't make him wait to be a writer till you're dead, Horace. It may be too late by then!"

Horace eyed Regner now with a half-fascinated disgust. "What exactly are you proposing?"

"That you give Douglas a million dollars. This very morning!"

Horace decided that the only thing to do now was to treat the whole matter as a joke, so he purported to chuckle and then noisily opened up his *Herald Tribune* between himself and his importunate acquaintance.

He was not, however, able to make sense out of a single sentence. He could not even read the captions under the photographs! At Grand Central he left the car without another word to Regner and hurried through the crowd to Vanderbilt Avenue and the now yearned-for security of his small office.

"Good morning, Mr. Devoe." Mrs. Sprit, gray, bland, plump, clad in reassuring black, beamed at him.

"Morning," he grunted as he passed her and almost fell into the big chair by his desk. He knew she would not disturb him till he had read his mail.

The reason, he was well aware, that he was so deeply disturbed was not that he had never considered Regner's idea, but that his determination to make Douglas earn his own living was part and parcel of a code that he had accepted as gospel from his earliest years. Indeed, the code had always seemed to him the only thing between himself and chaos. He had put his life together, piece by piece, like a mosaic. He had built a routine slowly but surely, blocking out anxiety with the water-tight compartments of his day- and night-filling schedule. He rose at the same hour, ate the same breakfast, greeted Amelia, who had hers in bed; spent the morning with Mrs. Sprit, the afternoon at one of his boards, the evening at the opera or a small dinner party. When it all worked in close sequence he was sometimes almost happy, particularly in the back of the opera box imagining himself as the tenor belting out "Celeste Aida." His life was like one of those palaces in Florence, all rusticated rocks and steel gates on the façade and all safety within. But when someone without a ticket barged in, someone like the wretched Regner, the whole place was turned to rubble, and in a flash!

His father, of course, had been just the opposite. The most hated trader in Wall Street had not given a damn for anyone's opinion; he had called the world a hypocrite and told it to go hang. Horace had not disapproved of his father or even resented him; he had simply envied him. But he had always known that he lacked the smallest spark of his father's fire and genius.

How else but by convention could he have faced the hate that his terrible sire had scorned? Hadn't he always known that he lacked the paternal armor, the paternal shell, and that to avoid the shrilled obscenities, the hurled brick-bats, he had to conform himself to just what the world thought was an acceptable rich man, a dutiful trustee, an admirer of the best things, a faithful husband (though that was easy, with the lovely Amelia) and a father who did not spoil a child?

Had he ever really thought of Douglas?

Had he ever really thought of Douglas as a person, not a son?

Hell's bells, it was too much!

"Mrs. Sprit!" he cried.

"Sir?" The pale face loomed in the doorway.

"Get me Mr. Curtis." He leaned over his desk and clenched his fists until he heard his buzzer. "Oh, Albert? Good morning. There's a matter I'd like you to take care of today. Yes, today. I want to settle a million dollars on Douglas."

A year later Horace was seated once again with the great investment banker in the club car. He had not seen Simon

Regner in the interim because the latter, to Horace's considerable relief, had taken his wife and a large family party on a grand tour in a yacht around the globe. But now, alas, he was back, and just as big and glossy and brassy as ever.

"Well, *well*, my dear Horace, how are things with you? And how in particular is our budding playwright? I heard he's gone to Paris. Is that so?"

"That's where people go to write, I'm told."

"They do other things there, too, *I'm* told!"

Horace averted his eyes from the other's grinning countenance. "Douglas's wife and children are with him," he retorted dryly.

"Of course I didn't mean a thing by that remark. Not a thing. I'm sure we'll soon be reading of a new Eugene O'Neill. And how is your lovely wife? You should take her on a cruise such as the one we've been on."

Horace could hardly repress a shudder at the prospect of further expenses. "Amelia and I are quite happy at home, thank you."

"Are you? May I be so bold as to remind you that I had a hand in the rehabilitation of Douglas Devoe? Why should I confine myself to the young? Should my benefactions not be showered alike on the older generation?"

It seemed to Horace that there was something almost Mephistophelean in the large confident figure in the adjacent Pullman chair. He could almost imagine the ho-ho-hos and ha-ha-has of the devil in Gounod's opera.

"I don't know that Amelia and I are in particular need of your benefactions. Of course, it's very kind of you —"

"You? I wasn't thinking of you, my friend. You seem as snug as that carpeted insect. No, it's Mrs. Devoe to whom I have the presumption to raise my sights. Has it never oc-

curred to you that you're a bit of an ogre? To keep the
reigning beauty of Park Avenue and Westchester County
so immured? Oh, you may immure her in palaces, but may
palaces not be prisons?"

Horace, once again transfixed by this monster, found
himself unable to be silent. "Prisons?"

"Everyone knows that you and Mrs. Devoe limit your-
selves to a small, select circle. I am sure it is very agreeable.
Certainly for you. It contains the friends you have known
all your life. But your wife, my dear Horace, was born to
reign! Both town and country yearn for her. She should be
the chairman of the Westchester Ball for the disabled; she
should be the one to greet the governor when he comes to
the music festival; she should open the new arts center
at —"

"Amelia doesn't want any of that!" Horace interrupted
sharply.

"My dear fellow, how do you know? How can any of
us read a woman's heart?"

When Horace reached for his paper and tremblingly
opened it, it was as if he were shutting out the rays of a
malignant force.

All that day his thoughts were in a tumult. He had never
doubted that Amelia was the idol of his life. She had been
so beautiful, in spirit as in flesh, that there had been no idea
in his mind of his money acting as any sort of attraction to
her; she was so far above him and above it that her love
had been a miracle. No fortune, no kingdom would have
been too great to lay at her feet. It was true, of course,
that he had rescued her father, a poor but dishonest broker,
from disaster; it was true that she had been twenty-eight
when they married and that foolish persons had spoken of

his being a great match. But all that he had been able to give her — the Palladian houses that so well set off her tall, cool, American beauty, the great garden in which she so tirelessly worked, the opera box from which, in intermissions, she was the cynosure of all eyes — was as nothing to the joy and pride that it had given him to devote his major energy to being an acolyte at the altar he was fortunate enough to have been able to build for her.

And it was almost more wonderful that Amelia, who had never seemed conscious of her beauty, who never gave herself any airs or sought to attract the attention of other men, should have been so serenely content with just what he offered: the unvarying routine of their households, the small dinner parties of old acquaintances, the opera and symphony. Amelia had a nature of remarkable equanimity; she never seemed to tire of her gardening, of her poodles, of her light romantic novels or of her husband. Sometimes Horace thought that she was like a wife in a dream. On the rare occasions in their married life when she had been subjected to the too emphatic admiration of some perhaps intoxicated male friend, her reaction had been first disgust and then pity. "I think Bill should really see a doctor," she would conclude.

The day of his talk with Regner was a Monday, and the Devoes were to be in town that week. Amelia came in in the afternoon in time for the opera, and Horace was plunged again in his nervous thoughts as he sat in the back of their box at *Norma*, his eyes on the straight back and beautiful shoulders of Amelia, erect and still in her corner seat in the front row.

"Casta Diva," he murmured to himself as Rosa Ponselle, before the altar on stage, delivered herself of the great aria. Had he kept the chaste goddess too greedily to himself?

When they came back to the house on Park Avenue, and the butler had taken their wraps, Horace told him to go to bed.

"I'll lock up, Johnson," he said. Amelia already had one foot on the staircase. "Oh, darling," he said, "don't go up quite yet. Could we chat for a minute?"

"Certainly, dear. What's on your mind?"

"Nothing much. I'd just like to talk."

She was already walking to the little reception hall on the ground floor where they never sat. Perhaps she was tired and did not want him to be too long. "How is this?"

They were both seated on stiff chairs that they had probably not sat on in twenty years, if ever. It seemed very odd.

"Amelia, do you ever think that our social life is too restricted?"

"No. How?"

"Well, we live in such a big city and see so few people."

"We can always add to the list. Whom would you like?"

"Oh, no one in particular. I was thinking more in terms of groups. Wouldn't you like to see some politicians? Or musicians? Or writers?"

Those serene gray eyes gazed at him the least bit more critically. "You mean *you* would?"

"No, no, I've been quite content, really."

"Are you sure?"

"Of course I'm sure."

"Then that's all I care about." She made a motion to rise. "Can we go up now?"

"No, no, just another minute, please, dearest. I've been wondering about something. Haven't I perhaps been keeping you too much to myself all these years? It seems almost oriental, when you stop to think of it, your being walled away like this, except for one dull little group."

"So you *do* find them dull?"

"No, no, no. How could the likes of Horace Devoe have the gall to find anyone dull? But *you*, Amelia. You were born to be a queen. To shine! And I'm beginning to wonder if I haven't committed a great wrong in keeping you so back."

"And does having committed this great wrong, as you call it, make you unhappy?"

"Well, shouldn't it?"

"Has it in the past?"

"I suppose it couldn't have, if I wasn't aware of it." He paused, perplexed, and then took another tack. "But maybe yes, it has. Maybe what I've all along been basically suffering from is a hidden sense of the injustice I've done you. It could be a kind of subconscious thing."

He was thinking so hard of this that in the silence that followed he did not at first notice that what was brightening her eyes was tears.

"Darling, what is it?" he cried in alarm. "I didn't deserve to be happy, did I?"

"I thought you did." Her voice was very sad and low. She had turned her head away from him. "You saved my father from suicide."

"But, Amelia, angel, that was all done with a check! And I got my money back, anyway. What man wouldn't have done that for the girl he wanted to marry?"

"I vowed I would make you happy," she went on in the same tone, shaking her head slowly. "I was determined, beyond everything, that I was going to make you happy. And I thought I'd had some success, too. That we'd had a good life. But now you tell me I've wasted all those years! That I should have been a society queen. That *that* was what you wanted all along!"

"Not what *I* wanted," he interrupted, horrified. "What I wanted for *you*. Or should have wanted for you."

"What's the difference? I didn't do what you wanted. I haven't been the woman you wanted. I've wasted my life. I've been ridiculous!"

Suddenly she began to sob, but when he hurried to her side she pushed him roughly away. He felt in that moment what it was actually to want to be dead.

"Whatever my life has been, dearest, it's been you!" he almost shouted.

"But what have I made of it, if that's true? No, Horace, let's not talk about it any more. It's too painful." She rose, putting a handkerchief to her lips. "I'm going to bed."

"Damn Simon Regner!" he shouted.

Amelia paused at the door. Then she turned back in surprise. "Why do you damn Mr. Regner?"

"Because he started me on all this. I was perfectly happy until he persuaded me that I wasn't. That I had wronged Douglas and was wronging you. Well, he was right about Douglas, so I —"

"Right about Douglas?" Amelia seemed now to lose all sight of her own discouragement. "You mean it was *he* who gave you that ridiculous idea of settling money on him?"

"Why ridiculous? Didn't it work?"

"Work? It has made him miserable! It has made him discover he has no talent for writing." And then, abruptly, another thought seemed to strike her. "But how did Mr. Regner know about Douglas? Did Douglas complain to him about money?"

"He told him he couldn't afford to be a writer."

"Then, Douglas deserves what he got!" she exclaimed indignantly. "Imagine whining to Regner!" And as she took in at last Horace's stricken countenance, it was as if the rehearsal of a dramatic scene had been interrupted, and the performer was herself again. Amelia took a step towards Horace, paused and then impulsively stretched out her arms. "Oh, you poor darling! I never meant to tell you that about Douglas. It was Elly who wrote me about it. I replied that of course he ought to go back to his old job, but she said it would look too silly now that he doesn't need the salary. Ah, now I *have* made you unhappy! Oh, Horace, can you ever forgive me?"

Six months later, when Simon Regner and Horace were again rolling towards the city in the club car, Regner asked, "What is this I hear about Douglas taking the chairmanship of the Turtle Bay Settlement House? Is he giving up Paris? I hope he's not giving up his writing."

"Let's put it that he wants to do something useful at the same time. Frankly, Simon, I'm not sure that Douglas needs that much time to write."

"His muse has dimmed, eh? Well, that happens. And we were sorry we couldn't induce your wife to be chairman of the Public Library ball. I had hoped that you two might be going to step out a bit more."

"We're quite happy, I guess, the way we are."

"And Simon Regner had better keep his big mouth shut, is that it?" Regner nodded vigorously to show how well he could take it. "Of course, I understand."

"No, I'm grateful for that big mouth, Simon," Horace replied with a new confidence. "Not so much for its effect on the lives of my wife and son as on my own."

"Oh? A salutary one, I hope?"

"Well, I don't think I'm going to tell you what it is. As you've gathered, I'm a rather private sort of person. But I will say this. You've helped me to see things that I hadn't seen before. And I think that's going to make me a better husband."

"But without any change in your life?"

"Without any outward change."

Simon Regner grunted and was silent. It was he this time who erected the protective wall of the *Herald Tribune*. But when he told his wife about the interchange that night at dinner her only comment was: "Those people are incredible, Simon. They're like crustaceans. Deprived of one shell, they'll scuttle about till they find an empty one. Anything, anywhere, so long as they don't have to *live!*"

America First

TIME HAD BEEN heavy on the hands of Elaine Wagstaff ever since she had abandoned her lovely pink house on the Avenue Foch and scuttled back to New York before the Nazi hordes. She used the word "scuttle" only to herself, for only to herself was she obliged to admit its appropriateness. She could never quite overcome the feeling that she should have stayed on and joined the resistance, though the resistance of a septuagenarian American widow would hardly have saved her beloved France. But wasn't there always an element of scuttling in any self-removal in the face of danger, particularly when so many brave friends were left behind? Elaine had hardly relished seeing the Rolls-Royce of the Windsors on the road before her; it was hateful to be identified with the international trash rushing to safer harbors to pursue their *dolce far niente*. Privilege in defeat makes for unlovable bedfellows.

This sense of unjust exemption from peril and hardship continued even more intensely after she was settled in the comfortable third-floor bedroom of her daughter Suzannah's brownstone of East Seventy-third Street, from the bay window of which she could gaze west to Central Park as she sipped her coffee on chilly fall mornings in 1940. Certainly she had to concede that Suzannah was doing her best to take the blame for that exemption upon her own square shoulders. Never in a long lifetime of being spoiled had Elaine felt quite so "nannied" as she did under her daughter's unceasing ministrations.

"But, Mother darling, no matter what you say, you've been under far greater strain than you can possibly realize. Oh, I've talked it over with Doctor Jennison! He quite agrees, and he has many refugees among his patients."

"I am not exactly a refugee, Suzie. I am still, after all, an American citizen, and not a poor one, either. It isn't as if I were costing anyone anything, and generous as you and Peyton have been — oh, generous to a fault! — I count on making it up to you."

"Oh, Mother! You know we'd never take a penny. Peyton would be mortally insulted."

"Well, we needn't dwell on it. After all, everything I have will soon enough be yours. It would only be robbing Peter to pay Paul."

"Mother, don't talk that way! You're going to live to be a hundred. Anyway, you've got to take it easy until you have your strength back. Crossing the Atlantic through submarine packs has to take a toll on the nerves."

Suzannah looked as if it would not have taken much toll on *her* nerves. She was all Wagstaff, all her father's child, with a round flat face, a tiny mouth and owlish eyes under thick black brows. Elaine never ceased to wonder that her own family, which had produced so many long-necked, slender beauties, so many "Boldinis," as the saying used to be, should have ended with Suzannah. But Suzannah, after

all, was fifty; she did not need allure. Would allure have
even suited the wife of a lawyer as important and unattractive as Peyton Priest? Elaine always thought of him
as grinning and bony, with thumbs under his lapels, a
Daumier caricature.

"You forget I came on an Argentine ship, darling. They
don't sink neutrals."

"Oh, don't they! Half the time they don't even know
what they're shooting. Peyton gets it all from his friends
in the State Department. And aren't I the lucky one to
have had all those wonderful trips abroad when I did! Do
you know I totaled up from my diary the number of times
I crossed the Atlantic with you? Thirty-two! Do you remember how you used to come to my cabin and wake me
up before dawn so we could be up on the bridge with the
captain and catch the first sight of land? No matter how
late you'd been up playing bridge or dancing, you'd always
be ready to stand with little Suzie straining for the first
glimpse of Europe!"

But no. Elaine readjusted the shawl on her shoulders as
if to shake off the cocoon in which Suzannah was trying
to envelop her. No, no, no. It hadn't been that way at all
on those voyages across the wintry Atlantic on the *Beren-
garia*, the *Olympic*, the *Majestic*. She had taken the little
girl out of school against everyone's wishes ("But, Miss
Chapin, you *know* she'll learn more French in Paris") and
left a hurt David to the obsessive pursuit of his decaying
business ("Darling, if you're too proud to live on my
money — *our* money, as I've always regarded it — if you
insist on wasting your life in a family business that hardly
pays the cook, then that must be *your* problem. *I'm* going
to Paris"). She had gone abroad year after year and had

finally bought the house on the Avenue Foch which, after David's death, had become her principal residence. She had been selfish, but at least she had lived, as the Wagstaffs would never have allowed her to had she knuckled under to them and stayed home. And she had preserved her marriage, too, such as it was; she had successfully reared her only child, such as *she* was. But she wasn't at seventy-five going to kid herself that it had all been a howling success.

Yet that was precisely what Suzannah seemed determined to make it, and, in her own way, always had. From her earliest years she had constituted herself as a kind of protector of both her parents. Daddy had always to be made to feel the successful businessman that he only too obviously wasn't, and Mummy, despite her globe-trotting, her frenetic social life, her passion for cards, her fear of boredom, had to be represented to the world as an almost compulsively loving parent who would give up the greatest party of the year to sit at the bedside of an even mildly ailing daughter. And when Suzannah screamed and threw tantrums about being left behind when Mummy went to Europe, wasn't it because of her child's insight that Mummy needed a chaperon?

And hadn't she? Hadn't little Suzie proved an effective one? Would Elaine have gone further with Rex Anders, or even with Guy de Vierzon, had Suzannah and Suzannah's governess (who could forget Miss Prunty?) not been in Paris? Perhaps, though she had been inclined to believe that it was more the warning example of her cousin Theodora, of just her age and looks and means, but who always went too far, much too far — she would read aloud to Elaine, with that piercing laugh, the worst tabloid extravagances about herself — that had kept her in line. Much as she had loved and admired and envied Theodora, who had sometimes traveled with her to Italy and Morocco, she could still see that a part of her value to her wayward cousin had lain in her own unquestioned respectability. The respectability of which little Suzie had certainly been a symbol.

Ah, what would Theodora, long dead now of a liver ailment, have thought of the war? What could she have thought of it but that it had made final ashes of the charred world that had been left of their youthful one after the ravages of its predecessor? Elaine shivered. Was Suzannah still talking?

She was.

"Of course, I don't expect you, darling, to spend all your time cooped up in the house. Fleming can drive you around the park in the afternoon and maybe over to Riverside Drive. And in another week or so we'll plan some little parties of your friends."

"Suzannah, I don't think, after what I've seen in France, I'm going to be in much of a mood for parties."

"Oh, I don't really mean parties. Just a few old pals in for supper. But perhaps you're right. Perhaps we should find something for you to do more in keeping with the times. You might even be interested in helping with some of my work."

"What sort of work is that?"

"I'm in an organization called America First. We're trying to rally antiwar opinion against Roosevelt's underhand efforts to get us involved in Europe."

"You mean you're against Lend Lease?"

"Well, not if it's really confined to that. We don't object to giving some help to England. We're not for the

Nazis — far from it! But what we don't see is why American boys should be sent abroad to pull England's chestnuts out of a fire lit by her own imperialism and stupidity!"

Elaine had often wondered what sort of a cause Suzannah would ultimately embrace, for she had always seemed made for one. But through the matrimonial years this large, somehow steaming girl had seemed oddly dominated by her sarcastic, grinning husband. Elaine disliked the very thought of Peyton Priest.

"I suppose a Nazi victory would be a very nasty thing," she ventured.

"But that won't happen. England can always negotiate some kind of stalemate. The point is that it's a European mess and should be solved by Europeans. England and France got us in once before, and what good did it do us? Or them, for that matter?"

"My poor France," Elaine murmured sadly. "If she has made mistakes, she is paying sadly for them."

"Mother, darling, I'm afraid you've always had a blind spot on the subject of the French. Yet deep down, I suspect you know how rotten their whole society is. New York is full of your titled friends who've fled the country they've betrayed and are now using the dollars of their American wives and mothers to buy the blood of *our* boys for their lost cause!"

Elaine blinked. Certainly Suzannah had a cause now! "Well, I must admit, my French friends did make rather a shamble of things. But I can only think of Edna St. Vincent Millay's poem about the lovely light shed by the candle that burned at both ends. Oh, I suppose you're right, my dear. Why should boys who've never known the beauties of France die for her? Did I?"

"Exactly! You wouldn't want to send Bert to fight overseas, would you?"

"Dear Bert. When will he come home to greet his loving grandmama?"

"Soon, I hope. I don't want him to cut any classes at Stanford. The draft only defers him while he's in school, and his marks have not been all they should be."

"The draft! Horrors. How close it all makes you seem to the war. But, of course, you're right. Bert mustn't fight for an old, decayed civilization. He's so *American*, Bert." Elaine wondered what her only grandchild looked like now. She had not seen him in three years. He had been a nice enough boy, but short and stout and, she was afraid, dull. "Yes," she mused, "what has Bert to do with all that? His life is *here*. His future is here." The memory of the Windsors' fleeing Rolls jarred suddenly upon her mental vision. What an idle life she had led! What a waste. What trivial occupations. And poor, awkward, unlovely Bert should die for all *that*? "Do you know, Suzannah, I think I'll look into this thing of yours. What do you call it? America First?"

"Oh, Mother, that would be so wonderful!"

Elaine did not find her tasks, when she took up the isolationist cause the following week, very demanding. She went to the large office leased by Suzannah's organization from a bank on Madison Avenue and helped to draft responses to letters inquiring about its goals. She was given a good deal to read, mostly in the form of newspaper and magazine articles. Elaine had never taken much interest in public affairs, but she had tended to take for granted, like most of her fellow expatriates, that America should oppose the Axis powers, even at the risk of war. Now, however, reading this new material with what she hoped was more an open than an empty mind, she found some of it rather persuasive. Mightn't it be better to let Germany win a round once in a while rather than having to send troops to Europe *every* twenty-five years?

But the real issue for her was Suzie. Here at last was something she could do for Suzie to make up for having been an indifferent parent. For the whole painful business of her repatriation had taught her to face up to her own deficiencies, at least in the maternal department. And poor Suzie had always been such an angel to her! Never once complaining about being made to feel a dowdy and un-wanted child. She would come now into her mother's tiny office two or three times in a morning (Elaine worked only in the mornings) to ask what she was reading and then hug her and cry: "Oh, Mummy, it's such *fun* our being together in all this!"

Suzie's intense preoccupation with her immediate family, Elaine decided, had to explain her attitude towards the war. For if Suzie adored her mother, she adored her son Bert even more. Bert must be kept alive, no matter what happened to the boundaries of Europe. And wasn't it pos-sible, Elaine wondered, that Bert might have been as cool a son as his grandame has been a mother? Why had he gone so far away to college if not to escape the tightness of Suzie's embraces? Suzie had always been determined to have a loving family around her, even if she had to create it out of the fevered workings of her own imagination. Had her father come back to earth, he would no doubt have been smothered with kisses and put to work in America First.

As Elaine's social life since her return to New York had been largely circumscribed by her daughter's, she had had little occasion to encounter the opposition in what was left of the old world of her friends and cousins to the cause she was now promoting. But one day, when she had decided for a change to lunch at the Colony Club, and was walking to a quiet corner of the members' dining room, she happened to pass a table at which some of her old acquaintances were seated, one of whom she instantly recognized as the recently arrived Marquise de Monrives, born Adelaide Stutz of Pittsburgh. Elaine particularly disliked Adelaide because of her appropriation, many years before, of Rex Anders, whom Adelaide had been willing to treat with far greater warmth, and she was disgusted to see her rival now, bloated, huge, with a choker of rubies and hideous purple eyebrows, laughing her high, shrieking abominable laugh, culminating in a screamed "Oh! Oh! Oh!" and apparently taking over Elaine's old New York circle. She quickened her step, only to be stopped by the marquise's direct address.

"Isn't that Elaine Wagstaff? Of course it is! Elaine, darling, don't run away. We were just speaking of you. Tell us the truth. Tell us that you've been libeled."

Elaine paused, smiling briefly at the others, considering, with perfectly justified smugness, that she was better preserved than any of them. "How have I been libeled, Adelaide? I must warn you, it may be perfectly true."

The table exploded in remonstrance, as if she had not been in jest.

"Oh, it can't be!"

"We won't believe it."

"Never. You, almost a *Française!*"

"What is it, girls?" Elaine demanded, surprised.

"They *say*," Adelaide murmured throatily, "they say, my dear, that you're . . . America First."

Elaine stared coolly at each of the five in turn. She finished with the Marquise de Monrives.

"And what are you, Adelaide? America Last?"

And she reveled in the quick stride of her own immediate departure.

She told Suzannah about the incident with pride; the latter was vociferous in her enthusiasm.

"Oh, Mummy, you and I are really together at last! I'm so happy. You're free of those horrible harpies."

But Elaine did not like this classification of her friends. "Adelaide I give up to you freely, my dear, but the others? I don't think you can call Florence King a harpy. Or Melanie Codman."

"Oh, maybe not exactly harpies. I guess I went too far there. But they belong to that international set that feels so much closer to London and Paris than they do to Chicago or Des Moines. And they wouldn't hesitate to shed American blood to save Eton or Oxford or the Comédie Française or the Grand Prix. They're not real Americans, Mummy. And now that I've got you away from them, after all these years, I'm damned if I'm going to let them snatch you back!"

Elaine was struck by the sudden idea that Suzie might be identifying all the things that her mother had preferred to herself in the past — parties in Paris, racing, gambling, beautiful people — with the Allied cause in Europe. It was as if Hitler were fighting high society and gaining an odd respectability by doing so!

"I think you'll find that many of the husbands of my friends had honorable war records."

"But don't you see, Mummy, back then it was the same thing! They were fighting for Anglo-French imperialism!"

Elaine was still too much alone in her new life to dispense with Suzie's support, but she began now to wonder how long she would need quite so many bristling turrets and machicolated battlements. Her daughter and son-in-law appeared to bring to the task of keeping America out of the war an animus against their opponents far bitterer than seemed required. Peyton Priest, like his wife, had little use for the survival of the kind of world that Elaine still wistfully missed and had perhaps too willfully loved. Indeed, he went further than she did.

"Suzie tells me you're really one of us now," Peyton told her that night before dinner, patting the hand into which he then placed one of his sugary rum cocktails. He looked at her with that guarded twinkle, that suspended husk of a smile, that was supposed to conceal, or at least cover, his distrust of all nonlegal minds and of female minds in particular. "I am very happy about that. You can now be our Trojan horse in the Colony Club."

"Don't you and Suzie go a little bit far there? Some of my fellow members are very intelligent women."

"Intelligent, my dear Elaine, of course! Have I ever denied it? My only point is that there are certain vital factors in modern life of which they are simply unaware. Because they exclude Jews from their society, they are ignorant of the force and organization of Jewish opinion. They are unaware, therefore, of the extent to which they are being manipulated."

"You think Jews are sinister?"

"I think that Jews, understandably, are more interested in destroying Hitler than we need be. It's a question, again, of what is and is not in our best national interest. I do not happen to believe that Jews put America first. Perhaps I should not myself, were I a Jew. But I'm not a Jew."

And glad of it, Elaine reflected, taking in that somber grin. She had been too inured to anti-Semitism in her long life to be shocked by it. She even tended to regard it, in some types of American professional men, as something naturally associated with their heaviness and seriousness. But in her international circles any form of ethnic prejudice had been considered "hick"; one couldn't be bigoted and "top drawer." Of course, in France she had met anti-Semites, but she was well aware that her son-in-law would have made little distinction between a Jew and a Frenchman. It was all rather confusing.

Peyton, at any rate, was only a source of mild amusement, or at worst of mild irritation. What really changed the quiet tenor of Elaine's existence and brought her up before the shooting pains of choice was a conversation that she had at the Colony Club with Erica Breeze.

Mrs. Alonzo Breeze, at least in Elaine's eyes, was the greatest social figure in Manhattan. Only ten years younger than Elaine, she was still the thinnest, daintiest, most elegant creature imaginable, and she wasn't afraid to wear large jewels or to tell you what she had paid for them. She had convinced herself that she was tired of the social whirl and sought only the divine peace of a quiet talk with a *real* friend — like whichever one she happened to be speaking to at the moment — and, what was more, she had the charm to convince that person it was true. She and Elaine were second cousins, but they had not met since Elaine's return to New York. Erica Breeze had the kind of visual intellect that can focus only on a person who is present. As with Louis XIV, out of sight was to be totally out of mind.

"Elaine, darling, I never *see* you! Are you often at the club? No, I get in here very little. My life has not been

much among women." Here she emitted a surprisingly
hearty laugh. Erica was very successful with hearty laughs.
"But what's all this I hear about your being an isolationist?
Are you really America First, Elaine?"

"Are you —?"

"America last? I know you said that to Adelaide. And of
course she is, was and always has been. But you, my dear!
You who have always so beautifully reminded us of our
debt to France! How can you tie yourself up to such a
bunch of dowdies?"

"Well, I can't help wondering why our young men
should die to pull England's —"

"Chestnuts out of the fire? Because they'll die in even
greater numbers if they don't. And to think of *you*, Elaine,
one of the loveliest, most glamorous things we've got,
rescued from all the horrors of war, only to be taken over
by those frumps! Why should they fear the Nazis? They're
as ugly as Huns." Again that laugh! "*Paris* is what they're
afraid of, not Berlin — anything that will show them up
for what they are. No, no, don't even talk to me about it —
I've neglected you horribly — imagine letting you fall into
such claws. I'm going to remedy things immediately. Come
to dinner. Tonight! I've got the most marvelous Free
French general and a secretary from the British embassy.
And all sorts of old pals of yours who keep asking, 'What
on earth has happened to Elaine Wagstaff?' Don't worry,
we won't quiz you about your horrible new friends. We
won't let you say a word. Just listen!'"

Elaine went that night to Erica's and had a glorious time.
She had almost forgotten what it was like to be among
people who cared so intensely for appearances, for things.

Dining at Erica's apartment, a veritable museum of impressionist painting, with her easily talking, easily laughing friends, was like swimming in a translucent Caribbean cove amid brilliantly colored fish over a sand as smooth as a rich carpet. It made Suzannah's world seem like the hustle and bustle of a Coney Island beach covered with bulbous women and white-limbed men in lumpy black bathing suits.

The talk turned to the war and England's ordeal. Nobody made so much as a glancing reference to Elaine's supposed convictions, and she listened at first gratefully, and at last avidly to all they had to say. By the end of the evening she was thoroughly ashamed of her work on Suzannah's committee.

She slept little that night, bracing herself for the disagreeable talk that she was bound to have with her daughter. It turned out even worse than she had anticipated. No sooner had she mentioned the fact, when Suzie came in to bid her good morning over her breakfast tray, that she had enjoyed herself at Mrs. Breeze's, than her daughter burst out:

"I suppose there was a lot of talk about how soon they could get our boys over there!"

"There was some talk of greater aid to England, yes."

"Like an immediate declaration of war?"

"No, Suzie, not that. I found Erica and her guests considerably more moderate than I find your friends."

"And so they won you over? In one evening? Just like that! Oh, Mummy!"

"No, dear, it was not just like that. I simply thought that they put the case against a Nazi victory very cogently."

"I knew it! I should never have let you go! I should have locked the front door and held you here by force." Suzie stamped her foot now in an alarming show of temper. "You're like a drug addict. All Mrs. Breeze has to do is give you a whiff of that old atmosphere, and there you are, back in the same old crowd, caught by the same old clichés, ready like Saint Peter to deny me, not three times, but thirty times three, three hundred times three!"

"Suzie! Must I remind you that you're speaking to your mother?"

"As if I could ever forget it! What have I tried to do all my life but *have* a mother? And, of course, you've always cared more for that crowd and all their drinking and gambling and love-making, than you've ever cared for poor dull little me! Oh, I know it, I've always known it, but I still had to try to save you from yourself and bring you back to decency and honor and patriotism. Well, I guess I must face the fact it's a hopeless task!"

"If it's a hopeless task," Elaine said with dignity, "I think you had much better give it up."

"Oh, Mummy, no!" Suzie clasped her hands beseechingly. "Don't listen to me. I'll still help you. Please! Give me one more chance."

But Elaine, contemplating the fat flushed cheeks, the wild eyes and the messy hair of her only offspring, felt nothing now but distaste. She had tried, God knows, and nothing worked. And what did it matter, really, if it did or didn't? Churchill and Erica were preferable to Hitler and Suzie. For once in life, anyway, good taste and morals could go hand in hand.

"I think under the circumstances, Suzannah," she replied in a tone of lofty sadness, "that it might be best if I moved to the St. Regis. I've trespassed long enough on your hospitality."

Suzie burst into tears. "Go where you want! I'm not stopping you. I was an idiot to think I could ever weigh against any part of your old life. Your old life? Hell, your whole life."

Elaine was very comfortable at the St. Regis in a delicious little suite looking over and up Fifth Avenue, and it was indeed delightful to be taken up again by Erica Breeze. She knew that Erica's sudden spurts of perfectly genuine enthusiasm for old friends whom she had somehow lost sight of, had to be taken advantage of in their brief heat. It was not that Erica would drop her when the spurt was over, but Elaine would then no longer be able to count on the daily invitations that poured forth while her stock was high. But by then Elaine would have had her chance to sink her own roots in Erica's Eden. It was all the chance she needed.

Elaine was featured at Erica's dinners at a martyr of the Nazi conquest, as one who had been flung, stripped and battle weary, on our shores and was now ready and qualified to plead the cause of the threatened old world to the still immune new one. She rapidly put together every horror story that she had heard in Paris, embellishing them a bit — who, after all, could, or would want to correct her?— and found that she could be quite effective on her feet, gazing wistfully over the heads of her audience as she told her brief tales. She had always had a hankering to act, and now she discovered that her low, grave, musical voice, with its slight tremulousness, could be used to good effect. She was able to convey the impression that she was imparting only a few drops of the sea of human misery in which she had come so near to drowning. And it was all in a good cause, was it not? Could one proselytize successfully without a bit of histrionics?

She had continued to see Suzannah for lunch once a week, and they had managed to keep the conversation on neutral topic. But after Elaine had joined the membership drive for Intervention Now, the pro-war organization of which Erica was a co-chairman, Suzannah had suggested dryly that it might be as well if they confined their communications to the telephone. And when Elaine started speaking in public even these calls were discontinued.

On the Monday following the Sunday of Pearl Harbor the offices of Intervention Now throbbed with a muted elation. Elaine foregathered with a few of Erica's co-workers in her poster-filled office overlooking lower Fifth Avenue. After a secretary had closed the door, they sipped a toast to victory from a pint of warm champagne that Erica had brought in her handbag. It might have been indiscreet to be seen as overjoyed in a time of national sorrow.

"No matter what this dastardly attack may have cost us," Erica assured them solemnly, "it will be seen one day as a blessing in disguise. Hirohito will have saved democracy despite his damned yellow soul!"

Elaine, on the way back to her desk, was informed she had a visitor waiting in the reception hall, and she found Suzannah staring sullenly at a poster of an anguished Polish peasant father holding up his murdered child. When she turned to her mother, Elaine was at once appalled by the flush on her checks and the hate in her eyes.

"Dear Suzie," she began falteringly, "we're all together now, aren't we?" And she held out doubtful arms as if to receive the prodigal.

The prodigal did not rush to them.

"I hope you're satisfied now!" Suzannah almost shouted. "Bert was on the *Arizona*."

"Bert? On the *Arizona*?" For a moment Elaine could not think who Bert was. "Oh, Bert!" she cried as it came to her. "But that can't be! Bert's in Stanford. Bert's not even in the service!"

"He wasn't until three months ago. But then he quit college and enlisted. As seaman second class. And do you know *why*? Because of you! Because of you and your murderous committee!"

"You'd better come to my room," Elaine murmured, as the alarmed receptionist arose. "It's all right, Miss Pink. This is my daughter."

"I'm not going a step further into this snake pit," Suzannah ranted on. "You needn't worry, Miss Pink. I don't have a gun or a bomb. I'm going to say what I came to say. It won't take me long." She turned back to Elaine. "My son read about you in the paper. He wrote me that if you could do what you were doing at your age, at least he could join up. And do you know what else he wrote me? That he was doing it to make up for what *I* was doing! That you and he had to wipe out my shame. My shame!"

"But, Suzannah, what have you heard about him? He's not hurt? He's not —?"

"Dead? Very probably. We haven't heard anything yet. How could we? But whatever it is, I hope you're satisfied."

"Oh, my poor child, how can you go on so? You're hysterical, of course. Let me take you home. Let me —"

"Keep your hands off me! This is what you've been after all my life, isn't it? To sacrifice everything, and everybody — Daddy, me and now Bert — to your bloody France! You might as well have cut the poor boy's throat."

And she was gone. Elaine hurried over to peer through

the glass pane of the door into the corridor while Suzannah waited, interminably, ridiculously, for the elevator. At last the doors opened, and she almost jumped into the car.

Elaine went back to her little office and sat at her desk and tried to think and not to think. The boy might not be dead at all. Suzannah was half crazed. Then she shook her head, as if to clear her mind of something that might destroy it if she couldn't. For what sort of grotesque fate was it that made her so fatal to this wretched girl she had never loved? No, no, she wouldn't think of it! Even if Bert were dead, wouldn't many young men have to die? Why should Bert Priest be exempt?

She would go in to see Erica in a minute. Erica would be charming and sympathetic, and there was a war to win, and they were on the side of the angels. Very well, they would act like angels! She should be able to sell a million war bonds as the grandmother of its first victim.

Portrait
of the Artist
by Another

T HE REPUTATION of Eric Stair, who was little
known at the time of his death in the Normandy in-
vasion of 1944, has grown steadily in the last four decades,
and the retrospective show this year at the Guggenheim
has given him a sure place among the abstract expressionists,
although that term was not used in his lifetime. Walking
down the circular ramp past those large imperial bursts of
color; those zigzagging triangles of angry red piercing areas
of cerulean blue which seem to threaten, in retaliation, to
encompass and smother the triangles; those green submarine regions occupied by polyp-like figures; those
strangely luminous squares of inky black, I wondered that
there could ever have been a time when Eric Stair had not
struck me as a wonderful painter. And yet I could well
remember myself as a fifteen-year-old schoolboy at St.
Lawrence's in 1934 staring with bewilderment at the daubs
of the new history teacher from Toronto who had turned
his dormitory study into a studio. Nothing could have
seemed stranger or more out of place on that New England
campus than an abstract painter who was rumored not even
to believe in God.

My bewilderment, at any rate, had not lasted long; I had soon become an admirer of the man without whose example I might never have become a professional painter at all. Not that I have become an abstract expressionist. Far from it. What, I wonder, would Eric have thought of my portraits? Would he have simply raised those rounded shoulders and grinned his square-faced grin at the sight of all those presidents of clubs and corporations, those eminent doctors and judges who make up the portfolio of the man sometimes known as a "board room portraitist"? "Jamie Abercrombie," I seem to hear him saying, "may have made it into the world of art, but he has certainly carted all his lares and penates along with him!"

What I suppose I shall never fathom, no matter how deeply I dive into the subaqueous caverns of the past, is the exact balance between benefit and detriment that I derived as a painter from my juvenile acquaintance with Eric Stair. If it be true that his example deflected me from the paths of banking or law, it may also be the case that, discerning early how much he could accomplish in the field of the abstract, I became too fearful of competing with him there. Maybe I slammed that door prematurely. Maybe I was too anxious, in confining my art to portraiture, to hide away in a world where Eric would never seek to follow or humiliate me.

And there is another thing. I can face it now I am growing old. Without what happened at that school might I not have painted the nude? When I cast my inner eye over the long gallery of my portraits, it strikes me how covered up the figures are, how draped and buttoned and tucked in, how expensively and colorfully added to, how bolstered and propped! Even my ladies in evening dress seem to reveal to me, in their alabaster arms and necks, in the exposed portions of their breasts and shoulders, how much more they are hiding from intrusive eyes. It has been said of Philippe de Champaigne that, being obliged as a strict Jansenist to eschew the flesh, he limited himself to ecclesiastical or judiciary subjects where all but the face and hands could be enveloped in voluminous robes, white or black or scarlet red. The peak of his great art was in the portrait of Cardinal Richelieu, where the sweeping cassock expresses the power and energy of the ruthless statesman. I have sometimes in preliminary sketches attempted to convey the character of my sitter in the suit or dress alone, as a kind of reverse nude. But that is as near as I ever come to it.

At any rate, all I can do is write down the facts, at least as they appear to me, and see if some kind of answer can be deduced from them.

I grew up with a feeling of "not belonging." Some people claim that this has become so common a social phenomenon that the rare state is that of the child who feels himself a square peg in a square hole, but in my case the psychosis may have been intensified by my being the youngest, smallest and most subdued of a clan of Abercrombies who were generally large and noisy, and by my own uneasy suspicion that even if by some trick of fate I should become a true Abercrombie, I'd still be a fraud. For I cannot recall a time when my family did not seem to be trying to look brighter and funnier and richer and more fashionable than they were. Or was that true of everybody in the years of the great depression?

Mother dominated us all, as a famous old actress will dominate the stage. She was plump and rackety and full of high spirits, and she adored company. Her rich auburn hair, which surprisingly was not dyed, rose in a high curly pile over a round powdered face with small features and popping black eyes. Mother was thoroughly unintellectual and unartistic; she read nothing but detective fiction, and she never tired of cards or gossip. What saved her from being banal was the quality of her affections; she loved people, and she loved to laugh with them and at them. She was the presiding spirit of the summer colony in Southampton; a watering place was her natural milieu. She would amble down the sand to the Beach Club, close to our shapeless, weatherbeaten shingle pile on the dunes, and then back; these two sites made up her summer universe, except, of course, for the houses in which she habitually dined. Poor Mother! When the depression obliged us to give up the brownstone in Manhattan, and she had to spend the winter months gazing out on the tumbling gray Atlantic, it was a hardship indeed. But her spirits never flagged. She always found just enough "natives" for her daily game of bridge.

It sometimes seemed to me, because my siblings so strongly favored Mother, that I should have inherited some of Father's traits, but I could never really believe this to be the case. Father did not seem to have many traits to bequeath; his function must have been completed when the queen bee had been fertilized. Yet he was not subservient to Mother. He acted more like an old and familiar employee, a kind of trusted but peppery superintendent whose management of the household was never challenged. Father was bald and stooping; he would gaze at us with watery eyes that seemed to anticipate nothing but irrational conduct that it would be his tedious task to clean up after. His other children took him entirely for granted; only I made an effort to establish a relationship with him, and here I failed utterly. When I would ask him questions about his boyhood and the problems of growing up, he would look at me as if I had inquired as to the whereabouts of the washroom. Human intimacy must have struck him as a total irrelevance.

I realize now, looking back, that some of my sense of our being on the fringe of society may have been justified. We were as "old" as many other families, but we were a good deal poorer than the average in the world to which we clung. Father, so far as I could make out, had nothing and did nothing, other than to sell an occasional insurance policy, and Mother's trust fund was woefully inadequate to pay the bills with which she was constantly dunned. Of course, our state was a common one in the depression, but when club dues and school tuitions were left unpaid while Mother continued to entertain and gamble, she and Father came in for some harsh criticism. And I was early assailed by the uncomfortable feeling that, because I was plain and unathletic, I could not claim the partial exemption from social contempt that my exuberant, party-loving older siblings, no doubt unfairly, achieved. I deemed myself hopelessly encased in the parental tackiness.

There seemed, at any rate, just enough cash (plus a partial scholarship) to send me to St. Lawrence's, and I entered that school with a sense of profound relief. Here, I hoped, I would not stand out as the child of my parents; I would be on my own. The whole tightly organized academy, with its ringing bells and hurrying boys, with everything happening at exactly the time it was supposed to happen, struck me from the start as a welcome proof that a world existed outside the papier-maché one of the Abercrombies, a "real" world, properly possessed of order and neatness, of heaven and hell. I found absolution in its regularity and blessing in its very sternness, and I became an overnight convert to the conservative social values that it enshrined. Even today, when I visit the school and behold the tall dark Gothic tower of the school chapel rise over the trees as I approach it from the railway station, I feel that actuality, even if it be a rather grim one, is taking the place of illusion.

St. Lawrence's was considered architecturally a handsome school. Some four hundred boys slept and worked and exercised in long Tudor buildings of purple brick picturesquely situated along a creek that wound its snakelike way through the landscaped grounds. Sometimes, particularly in spring, the place seemed to exude a rich, throat-filling emotion, but in winter, under rapidly dirtying snow and a hard pale sky, it took on a somber gloom, and the narrow mullioned windows put me in mind of Tudor prisons, of Tudor discipline, of pale, tight-lipped Holbein victims and torturers, of the ax and stake. Emotion was never light at St. Lawrence's; life was always earnest. I thought of Christ, as the near-mystic headmaster evoked him, the Christ of the passion, whose nails and thorns were far more than symbols, an elongated tortured gray body hideously twisted on the cross and illuminated by streaks of lightning against a weird, flickering El Greco background.

There was some hazing in the first year, but being small and inconspicuous and having learned early the art of protective coloration, I passed largely unnoticed and was able to make my early peace with the school. I became fascinated with the figure of the headmaster, Mr. Widdell, a tall, bony, balding, emaciated man, himself a bit of an El Greco, who preached sermons with such intense zeal that he alarmed some of the parents. It began to seem to me, listening to him, awestruck, on Sunday mornings, that he was the nearest thing to God I should ever experience, that for me it would be enough if he *were* God. And I rightly inferred that in his capacity of deity, as opposed to that of a busy and overtaxed headmaster, he would have as much interest in the one as in the many, that his love (yes, his love!) could include me as well as the faculty, the student body, the harassed Irish maidservants and the grave, slow-moving old men who took care of the grounds and were known to the boys as the "sons of rest." I had the nerve, or the inspiration, to take my doubts to Mr. Widdell himself.

"Yes, Jamie, of course, you can ask me any question you like. That is what I am here for."

I sat, a huddled little bundle of nothing, across the great square desk from the aquiline nose, those huge, glassy eyes. Between us was the white stainless blotter of his total attention.

"It is the commandment about honoring my father and mother, sir. I wonder if I can honestly say that what I feel for them is honor."

Mr. Widdell's gravity did not seem to deepen at this, and my confidence grew with this further assurance of omniscience. "Let me ask you just one thing, Jamie. Do you love your father and mother?"

"I love my mother, sir. My father doesn't seem to have much to do with love."

"But you have no aversion to him?"

"Oh, none, sir."

"Well, then, your case may not be as bad as you fear.

Love of one parent is a good start. Can you tell me why it is that you feel you cannot honor them?"

"It does not seem to me, sir, that they lead lives that I can honor. My father is occupied with very small things, like winding clocks and seeing the oil is changed in the car. And my mother plays cards and gossips. I mean, sir, that is *all* she does."

"But the commandment is not to honor their conduct, Jamie. It is to honor *them*."

"No matter what they do?"

"No matter what they do."

"Even if they're thieves and murderers?"

There was a gleam of something like a smile in those glistening eyes. "Hadn't we better wait till we get to it before crossing that bridge?" The total gravity, however, soon reestablished itself. "Seriously, my boy, you must consider that God expects of his children only what they can give and only in the way they can give it. Your father, in his daily maintenance of the household, and your mother, in the cheer that she imparts to others, may be doing more for God than you suspect. In any event, it is not for you to judge them. And not judging them, you will find that you can and indeed will honor them."

I left the presence on wings of elation. How easily did he dispose of my nagging problems! And, on his side, feeling that he had done something for me, the great man warmed to me. He always greeted me now, when we passed on campus, and I was on several occasions honored with the much coveted invitation to breakfast at the headmaster's house. I worshiped Mr. Widdell. It was as if I had died and gone to a paradise where everything fell into its proper place. God ruled us with an awesome benevolence, and under his sway all was for the best. Resentments and harsh criticisms of one's family were as unnecessary as they were presumptuous. How did one know that they, too, were not serving to the best of their capacity? Beyond the walls of the school lay a nation throttled in depression, but what did these few minutes of misery matter in the blaze of eternity? I learned from the headmaster that although it is our bounden duty to alleviate the sufferings of the human body, our first concern must always be with the soul. Perhaps too hastily I found myself willing to render unto Caesar just about anything Caesar claimed was his. I did not then understand that Mr. Widdell was different from me in that he had something of the saint in him and that to those who were less than saints his doctrine had pitfalls.

I had drawn pictures since I was a child, and now I took to sketching in earnest. I drew the chapel, the altar, the reredos; I made copies of the stained glass windows and illustrated biblical stories. Some of my things were reproduced in the school magazine, and I felt very holy indeed. I must have been quite unbearable.

It was in the fall of my fifth form and next-to-last year that Eric Stair, then aged twenty-five, joined the faculty of St. Lawrence's. He was a Canadian, from Toronto, an artist who had come down to New York to work on a mural in a bank, the contract for which had been canceled for lack of funds. Jobless and penniless, he had been recommended by the bank president, a St. Lawrence graduate, to fill a vacancy in the school's history department. He certainly did not seem the type for a New England prep school; he was short, heavyset and muscular, with a craggy face, small, suspicious, staring eyes and thick, messy red

hair. There was a rumor that Mr. Widdell had asked him
if he were willing to attend all chapel services and received
the answer that he was willing — if he didn't have to pray.
He was reserved and minimally polite, and seemed to look
about him at the boys and the school with a faint bemuse-
ment, as if not quite believing they could be true. But his
personality was strong; he had no difficulty keeping discipline. The boys knew a man when they saw one.

I had a double connection with the new master, for I
was in his dormitory as well as in his class of European
history. As I was very much of a "mark hound," seeking to
make up for my small stature and athletic nullity with high
grades, and as history had been my best subject, I was
inclined to show off in class discussions. Mr. Stair watched
me with a sardonic eye. He was not impressed.

"But Germany started the war, sir," I protested, when
he questioned the wisdom of the sanctions imposed at
Versailles. "She was greedy and cruel. The Kaiser wanted
to take over the whole British empire."

"And hadn't the British wanted to take it over?"

"But the British had it, sir!"

"Hadn't they wanted it before they had it? If coveting
empires be a crime, shouldn't we start our sanctions in
London?"

"Well, even if there were some wrong things about
acquiring their empire, haven't the British made up for it
by using it as a force for civilization and world peace?"

"How wonderful that I, a colonial, should learn the
glories of empire from a Yankee lad with a Scottish
tag!"

The class chuckled; I was deeply humiliated.

"But whether or not the Kaiser wanted to rule the

world," Mr. Stair continued, "I think we might find him easier to deal with today than this new chap, Hitler."

I could not avoid the temptation to reinstate myself in favor by impressing him with my special knowledge. "Quite so, sir. After all, the Kaiser was a grandson of Queen Victoria."

But the old queen's name did not have the magic with a "colonial" that I had anticipated.

"Is that so, Abercrombie? Well, let me ask you something. Do you know how many individuals were in domestic service in the United Kingdom when Victoria the Good breathed her last in 1901?"

"No, sir."

"More than two million. Does that tell you anything about the reign of the good queen?"

"Only that the stately homes must have been kept spick-and-span."

"Not a bad answer, Abercrombie. I can think of others."

When he gave me only a B on my paper on the influence of Colonel House on Wilson, an essay that I had entitled rather flamboyantly "Gray Eminence," and I protested to him, he replied:

"You see history too dramatically, Abercrombie. Your mind is full of kings and cardinals and royal mistresses. You must learn that it's also full of little people. Slaves. Serfs. Abercrombies. Stairs."

Stair did not advocate any political policies, domestic or international, in his classroom. Like Socrates, he simply questioned everything. But because a certain antiestablishmentarianism emanated from his very failure to enunciate or endorse any of the usual school values, he became popular with the more sophisticated members of my form, who saw in cultivating him a way of developing their own independence of home and academic rule, an independence that largely boiled down to the desire to indulge in activities neither permitted nor even possible on the campus: smoking, drinking and necking. Talking more freely than they could to other masters in Stair's study before "lights," they could at least pretend they were doing those things.

My own position with Stair was different. Because I was determined to make him give me better marks, I studied ways to please him, and I soon discovered that, for all his craggy integrity, he was not entirely immune to flattery. My genuine fascination at his utter freedom from all my hang-ups may have tempered the unctuosity of my approach and made me less objectionable. He was also amused by my drawings and in helping me to improve them. Although I could at first make nothing of the dots and squiggles of his own abstract designs, subjects of considerable mirth in our dormitory when he was not present, I was already enough of an artist to perceive that the few strong lines he would introduce into one of my sketches had radically improved it.

I was very much surprised and pleased when he asked me to sit for a charcoal sketch, although I could not help asking why an artist of his school needed a model.

"I do not limit myself to abstracts, Abercrombie," he retorted. "Every now and then I feel inclined to do a likeness."

"Why me, in particular?"

"Let's put it that I want to catch the spirit of this remarkable academy in which I find myself. As the headmaster is not an available sitter, I must seek the next closest. I think you may do very nicely."

I knew him too well now to take this as a compliment,

but I was nonetheless flattered to be considered the "spirit" of anything. Something, however, a bit more serious than his gibing came out on the second and final sitting.

Stair had a bad cold and was in a foul mood, something rather rare with him. I made the mistake of asking him why he thought me representative of the school.

"You're not," he snapped. "You're representative of what they're trying to turn the boys into."

"And what is that?"

"A man who believes in the whole bloody mess." He worked vigorously for a silent minute on his sketch, as if he were cutting me into slices. "For God, for country and for a small New England church school named for a minor saint roasted on the gridiron by Romans who, perhaps because of their very lack of imagination, may have had some small glimmer of reality."

"And the other boys don't believe in that?"

"They take it for granted, which is different. I suppose one can't really blame them. They're cooped up here nine months out of the year. Hardly a whiff of the great depression outside gets through. Their families are basically unaffected. Oh, true, they've had to give up a butler or an extra cook, or close down the cottage in Maine or the fishing camp, and a few, perhaps, have actually gone to smash, but they're mostly still rich — stinking rich in contrast to ninety-nine percent of the other ants in the heap. And I suppose it's only human not to give a damn about other humans. If their parents and teachers don't, why the hell should they? But you, my lad, are a different breed. You have some kind of pygmy sense of the misery outside the gates, but you resent it. You fear it. You're like my old granny in Toronto. You think the poor are poor because they drink."

"Aren't you being a bit stiff with me, sir?"

"I don't think so. And you don't have to 'sir' me when we're alone. Well, all right, you may not be as bad as my granny, but you believe in the upper classes. You believe the Royal Navy is keeping the peace, and the British tommy is preventing his little black and yellow brothers from killing each other, and that over here, in God's country, Mr. J. P. Morgan is fighting to keep the madman in the White House from wrecking the economy. Isn't that about how you see it?"

"Well, I certainly don't think everything's so fine in the Soviet Union."

"That's right. Win the argument by calling me a commie." He made a vigorous stroke now, as if he were slashing a line through my countenance. But he wasn't. A model was a model, however much of a fascist.

"Well, *aren't* you a socialist?"

"Never you mind what I am, sonny. I told the headmaster when I came here that I wasn't going to be political, and I shan't be. But that doesn't mean I can't prick an occasional bubble of self-satisfaction."

I was thoroughly angry now. If he wasn't to be "sirred," he could take potluck in the dialogue. "If anyone pricked yours, it might blow up the campus!"

Stair threw back his head at this and emitted a roar of laughter. "So you can bite back. Good. There may be hope for you yet." He paused, his head to one side as he contemplated his work. "Well, I guess that's it," he said in a milder tone. "Want to have a look at it?"

That look may have changed my life. For what I saw in that dark, brooding, huddled figure, drawn with amazing power in so scant a number of strokes, was something more than the fear and the resentment in the features. These emotions I had known about. What I saw for the first time was the intensity of concern in the eyes fastened on the painter. The boy was alive! Alive as the painter was alive! It had never occurred to me that I was alive. And it had certainly never occurred to me that a painter obsessed with geometrical figures that were never completed, lines that went nowhere and dots that floated in limbo, could be the one to prove my existence. "I am in a Stair drawing," I could murmur after Descartes, "therefore I am!" I knew then and there that I was in the presence of a great artist.

From now on I attached myself, as much as the school schedule permitted, to Eric Stair. Perhaps because he regretted the harshness of his strictures on one so young, perhaps because every man has a corner in his heart for a worshiping slave, a devoted spaniel, he tolerated me. He even allowed himself at times to be amused by me. And he gave me serious instruction now in my art.

The headmaster, the angels, the glory of God, disappeared in a clap of thunder like Kundry's castle in *Parsifal*. I made desperate plans in my mind — not daring to tell my family — of skipping college and going straight to art school. And then there came a chance of actually introducing my new hero to my family.

Mother and Father never came up to school, but in the Easter vacation of that year they had received the loan of a large apartment in New York from a cousin of Mother's, and all the Abercrombies moved joyfully into town. I had a room with two beds, so I could have a guest, and when I heard that Mr. Stair had no place to go over Easter and was planning to stay at the school, I made bold to invite him to come to us. He accepted, with evident surprise, but with alacrity. I did not know at the time that he had a girl friend in New York.

He and Mother hit it off immediately. I was rather disgusted to note that she seemed to be actually flirting with him! They both showed me sides of themselves I had not seen before: Eric lost his sardonic, superior, detached school air and was full of chuckles and slightly off-color jokes, while Mother showed a concern about modern art and letters that I had not previously suspected.

"Your ma likes a man around," Eric told me one morning when we were alone at breakfast. "She hasn't totally forgotten she's a woman."

I was a bit shocked. "Why should she? She has Father."

"What is it they say? Thirty years is a long time with the same piece of meat?"

"If you're implying, Mr. Stair, that my mother —"

"Isn't dead below the waist? Yes, I am, my friend. Of course, no son can abide the idea that his mother is subject to sexual urges. But that doesn't mean she's neuter."

I was startled by this idea of Mother, so stout and matronly. But my respect for Eric was all-encompassing. What I minded far more than the impertinence of his suggestions was the ease with which Mother had taken him away from me.

He was not, however, as it turned out, discussing sex — or even the fantasy of it — between himself and Mother. He was discussing sex between himself and somebody else. What Mother was doing, incurable romantic (like so many gossips) that she was, was persuading him to marry his girl friend then and there and present the headmaster, at the beginning of the spring semester, with a fait accompli. And she succeeded. One morning at breakfast, as she beamed at him down the table, Stair announced to my bewildered and disapproving self that he and I and Mother would be going at noon to the Municipal Building, where he was to be joined in wedlock to a Miss Janice Hart.

Mother had not met Miss Hart, and even she was a bit disillusioned when we encountered this handsome, marble-faced, raven-haired, and only too evidently efficient and officious young woman in the little lavender room where the godless marry without benefit of clergy. Miss Hart would have given the back of her hand or worse to a priest. She greeted Mother and me in a clipped, perfunctory manner and proceeded to take over Eric and instruct him on what had to be done as if he were a tousled schoolboy and she a matron who could spare little time with recalcitrant pupils. When we repaired to our apartment afterwards to drink a bottle of champagne, she offered a mock toast to the school whose faculty family she was about to join.

"To St. Lawrence's Academy for conspicuous consumers!" she announced in a loud clear tone. "May we help to move it into the twentieth century!" Then she turned to Eric. "Or must we get it into the nineteenth first?"

What did he see in her? Or she in him? I suppose he saw a splendid figure possessed by a woman able and willing to dedicate it to his sexual delight. And I suppose she may have divined in him the artistic genius that she hoped she would one day be able to harness to the Communist cause. For that she was a Communist I had little doubt, even if she did not carry an actual card. She was committed, I felt sure, not only to the overthrow of the government by force but to the overthrow of just about everything else. Certainly she was willing to overthrow Mother and me, bidding farewell to the former with a casual: "Thanks, old dear; you made an admirable Cupid," while pulling me aside and whispering in my ear an anatomical precaution against the presumed sexual aggression of other boys at St. Lawrence's.

Mr. Widdell was startled, no doubt, when Eric arrived at school with a wife, but he declined Mrs. Stair's offer to stay at a local inn while her husband continued to manage his dormitory, and provided them with a tiny vacant apartment in the house for visiting parents, filling Stair's dormitory position with a bachelor master. The faculty and wives were no doubt astonished by Janice's personality, but she behaved herself better than might have been expected, was decently civil to all and spent most of her time in her apartment working on what we much later found out was a tract against the crimes of private education in New England.

The Stairs, of an occasional Saturday evening, would ask some of his old dormitory boys to drop in for cider and cookies, and on these occasions Janice showed herself more relaxed. She enjoyed twitting us about our "plutocratic" backgrounds while Eric puffed at his pipe and sardonically listened. With me, however, she was distinctly less friendly, her woman's intuition having already gleaned that I had the presumption to dispute her absolute ownership of Eric.

One night when she was descanting on the glories of the Russian revolution, I expressed horror at the brutal massacre of the czar and his family.

"Well, you've heard about making omelets and what it does to the eggs," she snapped.

"I don't see how any omelet could be worth gunning down those four lovely daughters and that poor little boy."

"Oh, that bothers Jamie, does it?" she asked sarcastically. "It distresses him that four spoiled brats and a hopeless bleeder should bite the dust? I won't say anything about Papa and Mama, for I guess even you might concede that a couple so bigoted and harebrained as to turn their country over to a crazy monk deserved what they got. Oh, sure, I'd have spared the kids. But what the hell difference does it make, weighed against centuries of injustice, starvation and torture?"

My dislike of my rival helped me to say what would most infuriate her. "You believe, then, that two wrongs make a right?"

"I believe that the undesirable classes do not eliminate themselves!"

"And you, I'm sure, would make a clean sweep of everyone at St. Lawrence's."

"No, I'd pick and choose. But I think I'd start with a snotty kid from Long Guyland."

Now her husband had had enough. "Oh, dry up, Janice. That'll do for Russia for one night. Go home, boys."

On another evening we had an even sharper clash. It was after a forest fire that had come close enough to the school to necessitate the faculty and students joining the local firefighters and members of the recently formed Civilian Construction Corps in combating the blaze.

It had been a startling experience for me. Never before had I been thrown into the company of a large troop of men, most of whom came from what my father called the "lower orders." As the area in which we were stationed was not touched by the fire, which had been brought under control after only a few hours, we had nothing to do but stand about and listen to the men talk. Talk perhaps is not quite the term. What I heard up and down the hillside and across the field where we were scattered was the exchange of obscene words, creating a kind of buzz across the countryside, like a swarming of bees. It seemed to me that all the men about me were talking at once, that nobody was listening, that there was no thought to communicate, that it was rather a litany that was being chanted, even a kind of bead-telling, that their sentences, insofar as they were sentences, were only nouns strung together to give a reason to filthy adjectives. At first I thought they were trying to shock the schoolboys, but at last I realized that I was being initiated into the habitual discourse of young male America.

When I told the Stairs about it, Eric, who had been out with us, was amused.

"Come on in," he grunted. "The water's fine!"

But Janice was odious. She put her arm over my shoulders in mock sympathy.

"Was little Jamie-Wamie shocky-wocky by bid bad men? Did they talk too dirty-wirty?"

I shook her off, furious. "It's not a question of being shocked. Although, yes, I was shocked. But what shocked me was how those men stripped every bit of natural color and beauty out of the whole countryside. They turned it all to a revolting brown."

"If you mean shit, why don't you say shit?"

"Because that's just the point! I *don't* want to say it. It's saying it that makes it that, don't you see?"

"I guess I don't see, honey."

"You don't see anything!" I cried, released at last by my fury. "And you couldn't if you tried. What a person to be married to a painter!"

"Go home, Abercrombie," Stair snarled.

"And good riddance!" his wife added.

"Let the kid be," he told her sharply, and it pleased me, as I left the room, to think they might be going to have a real row.

But if I thought I was going to improve my position with Eric Stair, I had a lot to learn about marriage, or at least about marriage in its first year. Eric, I think, had a certain tenderness for the boy who admired him as I did, but he was not going to allow this to get between him and the angry, passionate creature whom he possessed every night. If Jamie Abercrombie had to be sacrificed to her jealousy, he could only shrug his shoulders and comply. And, after all, Jamie Abercrombie *was* a bit ridiculous, wasn't he?

Why did she object to me quite so violently? I suppose because she begrudged the smallest patch of the territory of Eric Stair to anyone else. Had I paid my court to her, had I pretended to be a convert to her radical views, she might have allowed me a few square inches of Eric, provided she could have them back on demand. But she correctly read the resistance, nay, the hate, in my sullen gaze; she wanted to kick me, as a cat-hater wants to kick the small black creature, humped up and staring, that she knows she can neither win over nor fool.

It was now that I developed my theory that Janice Stair was a fatal presence in her husband's artistic career. If she had originally conceived the idea that she might convert his brush and palette into tools to further the proletariat revolution, her jealousy now saw in them mutinous soldiers conspiring to thwart her absolute rule. I had noted her hostility to abstract art. Of course! How can one arouse the downtrodden with dots and lines? I began to indulge in fantasies in which I would bravely face up to Eric's fury

and denounce her machinations to him, confident that after
the raging storm was over, the broken bedraggled man, a
drowned Lear or fool, would seek the humble hut of Jamie's
forgiveness, clasp one of my hands in both of his large ones
and murmur: "You've been a good friend, my boy. I see
it now. Oh, I see it all!"

And then came the terrible time when a quirk of fate
placed it in my power to convert my fantasy into a grotesque reality. God knows how different my life might
otherwise have been. Or does he?

Our dormitory, placed in what had orginally been intended for a large attic, had a curious zigzag shape, and my
cubicle, at the very end, had a window that looked out, as
did none of the others, on the visiting parents' house, so
that the window of the Stairs' bedroom, on the same level,
was only some sixty feet away. One night after lights, just
as I was dropping off to sleep, I heard a step on the floor
by my bed and sat up quickly to make out a pajama-clad
figure standing there. I was about to hiss an angry "I don't
play dirty games, thank you," for I was intensely puritanical about certain boarding school practices, when a voice
whispered:

"Let's see if we can't see Mrs. Stair's bare ass."

It was Tommy Agnew, our dormitory prefect, a sixth
former and captain of the football team. He sat down in
the chair by the window to stare into the lit but empty
interior across the way, and I sat up politely for a time
with him. Any interest in female anatomy was considered
sacred, and besides, he was a prefect. At last, however, I
grew tired and fell asleep.

The next morning, in the washroom, while brushing our
teeth, I asked Tommy if he'd had any success.

"Well, not for hours," he complained, as if he'd suffered an actual injustice. "I thought those people would never go to bed! But when they did, yes, it was worth it." Agnew paused to expectorate into the basin. "That woman doesn't even use a nightgown. Or at least she was bare-assed when she came to pull the shade. Jesus, what tits! And before she pulled the shade down, she gave a sort of sexy twitch of her ass. I think she may have suspected some boy was watching."

"That was generous of her," I observed sourly.

Tommy's information agitated me greatly. All that day I was in a kind of fever. How did that slut dare to intrude her naked loins and breasts and buttocks into the sanctity of a male church school? My mind fulminated with biblical anathemas, and I heaped logs on the crackling fire of my fantasized plans to rescue Stair from his whore of Babylon.

That night I anticipated a flood of visitors to my cubicle to share in Tommy's discovery, but there were none. The sole sixth former in our dormitory, he must have disdained to share his confidence with juniors, and his own form mates were not allowed in our quarters after lights. Tommy himself, presumably exhausted from his vigil of the night before, did not appear, and I sat by my window in the dark alone.

I think it must have been midnight before she appeared. I had not really thought she would. But she did, and I was choked with hatred and a kind of dizzy lust. When she raised her arms to the shade her fine, large firm breasts jutted at me like two celestial cannons, and, distinctly, before she pulled the curtain she twitched her marble hips. I felt she was looking at me directly, defiantly, imperiously, devastatingly, destroyingly. Then the black shade descended.

That morning I awakened an hour before the rising bell and sketched my memory of that nude figure framed by the window. I worked furiously for the sixty minutes, and I wonder to this day if it wasn't the best thing I've ever done. At the sound of the bell, which almost terrified me with its harsh, jangling, puritanical interruption of my heated and frenetic endeavors, I rose and placed it in my sock drawer. There it was almost sure to be discovered by the snoopy and prudish bachelor, Mr. Morse, who had taken Stair's place as our dormitory master and who was known to investigate both our beds and our bureaus.

Mr. Widdell did not delay in doing what he had to do. He reached into a manila folder, pulled out my drawing and laid it on the desk so that it faced me. "We won't play games with each other, Jamie. Mr. Morse discovered this in your cubicle and thought he had better bring it to my attention. It shows, I believe, a considerable talent. But the subject is not one that I feel is suitable for your art work. Perhaps later, when you are an adult. I believe there are such things as 'life classes' where you can draw unclad models. But this picture seems to me to have emanated from a fevered imagination. If you have such thoughts, I think you should take more physical exercise. I should like your permission to destroy the drawing, and your promise that you will not reproduce it."

"But it didn't come from my imagination, sir."

"How could it not have? You can't mean that there was a model in the school? And I cannot believe that your parents would have permitted you to attend a life class in vacation."

"No, no, sir, it was something I saw, here at school." I leaned my head over the desk, staring down at its surface, as if struggling with a terrible embarrassment. "I hate to say it, sir, but I don't want you to think that I have a fevered imagination."

In the awful silence that followed I at last looked up. Mr. Widdell's face was stricken with incredulity and dismay.

"You mean, you saw a woman unclothed? *Here* at St. Lawrence's?"

"Yes, sir."

His voice now rose to a bark. "Are you telling me, Abercrombie, that you've been a peeping Tom?"

"No, sir! Please, sir!" I burst into tears. The sudden terror at what I was doing must have had the effect of grief. "I didn't peep. She was right there by the window. For a long time, just like that. She stood there, looking out at the night, and I had plenty of time to study her. I didn't think it was wrong, sir, I thought it was like an art class, as you say, sir."

"She? Who?"

"Mrs. Stair, sir."

"You say you saw Mrs. Stair in that condition? At night?" In the silence, as I waited, I could see that he was mentally correlating the windows of the Stairs' apartment with the windows of my dormitory. "At what time of night?"

"I don't know, sir. It was after lights."

"You shouldn't have been looking out the window. You should have been asleep."

"I know, sir. But I couldn't sleep. It was a warm night, and I got up to sit in my chair by the window."

The headmaster, obviously much agitated, snatched up my drawing and tore it in two. "That will be all, Jamie. We will not speak of this again. You did wrong, but it is understandable. Let us have no more night peerings."

I hesitated as he simply sat there, glaring at me. "Will that be all, sir?"

"That will be all."

"You won't tell Mr. Stair, sir? I mean, he might not understand."

"I shall not mention your name. Now go."

Nobody, including myself, knew just why the Stairs left the school the following week. The headmaster's version — that Mrs. Stair was faced with a serious illness in her family — was believed by no one. It was obviously most unusual for a master and his wife, both apparently in perfect health, to quit before the end of the academic year, with all the trouble to the school of replacing him in his courses, and the enigma was deepened by the fact that the Stairs said goodbye to nobody. They simply disappeared.

Years later I learned that Mr. Widdell had informed Eric that he and his wife were to be moved immediately to a hotel in the village until a new apartment off campus could be found for them. When Eric had, quite naturally, insisted on a reason, the headmaster had simply replied that Mrs. Stair had been seen by boys in a state of undress at her window. When Eric had demanded indignantly if the headmaster was suggesting that his wife had intentionally exposed herself, and had received no answer, he did the only thing a gentleman could do: he resigned his post after threatening to punch his superior in the nose.

What I did, I suppose, was to suppress, in the psychiatric sense, the whole matter. I simply decided, in the panic that threatened to overwhelm me, that I had to dismiss the subject as far as possible from my mind. I affirmed to myself that there was no necessary connection with what I had wanted to accomplish, that is, the opening up of Eric Stair's eyes to the kind of women he had married and his sudden detachment from the world in which I lived. I was confident that the headmaster had not disclosed the fact of my artifact; he had, in fact, destroyed it before my eyes. And he never thereafter alluded to the topic. I banished the Stairs from my conversation even at home, responding curtly to Mother's inquiries, and in time I almost came to believe that the episode had not occurred, though I would sometimes wake up in the night with the memory of a nightmare and then, while I was waiting for that soft re-assuring feeling that it was all a dream, the horrid notion would steal into my consciousness that it was all too true, and I would jump out of bed and walk briskly to and fro, desperately trying to convince myself that I had blown up the whole matter monstrously out of proportion.

In time I learned to live with myself, and as the years at school and then college passed, it became almost a quaint recollection, like some childish prank that one could tell people about with a smile, even when it was a fairly nasty one. Only I didn't.

Eric had begun to make a name for himself. He had a studio in SoHo, and some of his paintings had been shown at the Whitney and the Museum of Modern Art. I started gradually to allow myself to think about him again, and I would inquire about him, when I was with art enthusiasts who had no reason to suspect that I had known him. I was very excited when I learned that he and Janice had split up and that she had married an active member of the Communist party. Perhaps my now ancient crime had been for the best!

After my graduation from Harvard in the spring of 1939 I came to New York to study at the Art Students League. I determined to call on Eric at his studio, and when I did so, I was cordially received. He occupied a large loft filled with his huge abstracts and seemed contented and cheerful. He acted as if we had parted the day before and did not show the smallest surprise that since our last meeting I had become a man.

After several drinks and much talk of his painting and of mine — he charmingly treated me as an equal — he made a startling suggestion.

"How would you like to take over this studio while I'm gone?"

I looked around me. "But where are you going?"

"I'm going home to sign up. I'll be leaving in a day or so."

I was astonished. Of course, he was a Canadian and of course the war in Europe had started, but somehow I had thought he had joined his destiny with ours.

"You look surprised. I suppose you're recalling that I had it in for the empire." His chuckle seemed quite devoid of partisan feeling. "Well, this war should finish it, anyway, whoever wins. And no matter how I feel about the stately homes and the British Raj, I have to back them against the bad boy in Berlin."

"But your art, Eric!"

"Who gives a blow about art, dear fellow, when the world's on fire? You'll find you'll be coming in yourself. And the beautiful portraits of Jamie Abercrombie will have to wait!"

At that point, a terrible thought struck me. If he and Janice had still been married, they might have had a child or children! He might have had to stay and support them. I leaped to my feet, clapping a hand over my mouth.

"What is it, Jamie? Have you seen a ghost?"

"Yes! Oh, my God!" In that moment I was absolutely convinced that he would be killed. And whose fault would that be? "Eric, I've got to tell you something. I've got to make a confession."

My sorry tale erupted from the mental storage closet where it had been so long and securely kept like a short story read aloud by a proud author, without an "er" or an "ah," in finished sentences. But the author was far from proud. What would Eric do? Would he strangle me? He was strong enough. That craggy face was absolutely expressionless, but I thought there was a glimmer at last of something like amusement in his small blue eyes. When I finished there was a moment's silence. Then he whistled.

"My God, it's like something out of Kraft-Ebing! Those schools should be suppressed."

I stared in disbelief. "Then you don't resent me? You don't think I'm a fiend?"

Eric looked at me with faint surprise. "No, I don't resent you, Jamie. I've made my own life, such as it is, and I've left St. Lawrence's a good way behind me, just as I've left Janice. So none of it matters to me any more, except that it's amusing. But for you, yes, I guess I can see it's another kettle of fish. Because you have to face the fact that you behaved like a real shit. And there may be some of that shittiness still in you."

How he said that! As pleasantly and with as much detachment as if we'd been discussing a character in fiction. Of course, that made it all the worse. To my own astonishment and shame the tears that I had not shed five years before and that may have been waiting for just this summoning flowed forth, and I found that I was sobbing.

"Jamie, Jamie, my poor fellow," he said, putting an arm around my shoulder, "let it come out — it will do you good. I'll write you from time to time. Just to show you that I'm all right. And that just because you were a shit once doesn't mean that you always have to be one."

I pulled myself together at last, and we went out to dinner and talked of St. Lawrence's until the small hours. He was very funny and mercilessly observant. It seemed there was nothing on that little campus that had escaped his painter's eye. I drank far too much, and he very kindly took me home in a cab. But the next day when I called to thank him he was gone.

He did write me, every few months, during the war, and I received his letters at the Pacific base where I was stationed. Without the mercy of this correspondence I think I might have been emotionally crippled when the news of his death reached me in the summer of 1944. As it is, I have never since been able to draw or paint a nude figure of either sex.

No Friend like
a New Friend

WHEN STUART DIED — in part, Frances Hamill always believed, owing to the exhaustion of arguing no less than three major cases in the 1960 winter term of the U.S. Supreme Court — it seemed to her that her life also was over. What remained would be as gray as the ashes of an Indian widow who has committed suttee, a dignified passivity, a kind of subdued suspension of any real living. She was perfectly aware, if with a certain complacency, that she was hopelessly out of date and fashion, that she lived in an age of wedding feasts supplied with funeral baked meats, that the relict was supposed to prove that her marriage had been happy by contracting another in a year's time or less. But she cared nothing for any of this. She had been Mrs. Stuart Hamill from the age of twenty-three to that of sixty; her two daughters were married and settled; she had her memories, her dogs and her books. It should be enough.

It might even have been greedy to want more. How many individuals among the starved and tortured millions who had populated the planet since our cave ancestors, had enjoyed a fraction of what she had enjoyed? How many had her health, her love, her amusements? How many women had been happily married to a husband who had been a great lawyer, a great banker, an adviser to presidents?

But it was one thing for Frances to consider that her real life was over; it was quite a different matter when others came to the same conclusion. Her daughter Leslie had the tactlessness of many women married to tactful husbands. The pretty dark neatness of her perhaps out-dated femininity tended to harden in mother-daughter "chats" where her self-interest was not always successfully concealed.

"You know, Mummy, one thing that you'll have more time for now, and that may act as therapy for you, too, is really getting to know your grandchildren. Oh, I admit you've been a marvelous gran, of course, but I mean something deeper. You could take Alison abroad, for example, for her spring vacation. It would be a great treat for her. And for you, too. She's a brilliant girl; doesn't miss a trick."

"But I don't think I want to travel just yet. I know that widows are expected to be in orbit half the year. I'll get there, but give me time, dear."

"Well, of course, you don't have to go anywhere. You could have the grandchildren with you in Bedford. You could let them have their friends out, too. House parties of young people! Oh, I don't mean yet, naturally. But in time. After all, you'll be rattling about in this big house. You'll be glad to have people to fill it up."

"I shan't rattle, Leslie. Your father was not such a large person that his absence will make that much difference. Though I suppose it may be difficult to justify the expense of so big a place for one old woman." Frances waited in vain for Leslie to deny this. "I suppose you think I should sell it and make gifts to you all."

"Well, isn't it foolish to let the estate taxes eat everything up? Have you talked to Polly about it?"

Frances thought, with a sudden rip in her heart, of Stuart's smile and the gentle whine of his "Ah, now, Leslie." He always said that Leslie was unchangeable, and never tried to change her; he would simply register the mildest notification that he had noted. He was before Frances now in one of those moments of striking vividness that happen in the first weeks after a death, that almost induce a belief in ghosts. She reached out a hand as if to touch him; Leslie did not even notice. Yet there he stood, tall and stocky, his hands in his pockets, his head cocked to one side, his lips fixed in that noncommittal grin, his small, twinkling, piercing blue-gray eyes full of that constant attention, that benevolent, all-taking-in attention, that sometimes terrible attention. How was it, Frances found herself suddenly wondering, that his tonsure of curly gray hair made one forget that his scalp was bald? Perhaps that was part of his greatness, she thought. Or was that sarcastic? Could Stuart read her mind? But if he could, if he knew what she was thinking, then he had to know everything, and if he knew everything, it was all right.

"Stuart, I love you," she whispered to herself. "You know I love you. You've been my whole life."

Leslie still did not notice.

Polly was almost the opposite of her sister Leslie. Polly was a partner in Stuart's law firm. They had a policy against nepotism, but they had broken it in her favor because they had decided the time was coming when they would have to have a woman partner, and they wanted one whom they could "trust." Polly was in charge of Stuart's estate, and she handled Frances's matters, too, and, perhaps because she was a lawyer with a good income of her own, perhaps because her nature was more generous than Leslie's, she was less concerned with how much Uncle Sam would get when her mother died. Yet Polly in her own way could be quite as irritating as her older sister. The bright yellow eyes behind the wide, gold-rimmed glasses snapped at Frances as she tapped the end of her thin gold pencil against her large, fine, front teeth. There was something faintly defiant about her smallness, her neatness and her prettiness that seemed to say: "Oh, yes, I can beat you at any game. You name it. We'll play it."

"Jim and I think you ought to do more things with your hands," she told Frances. "He's taken up basket weaving on weekends. You should see what he's done. It's really remarkable."

"But I've never been able to do anything with my hands. As a child I couldn't even draw a moon face."

"You could learn. There are all kinds of classes. Pick a craft. I'm serious, Ma. We're all too eye-oriented. If you suddenly found you couldn't read, your life would be empty."

"What would yours be?"

"There are blind lawyers. I could learn braille."

"And couldn't I?"

"It's harder when you're older."

"I think I'm going to take my chances the way things are. Without basket weaving."

"I'm only trying to help, you know."

"I know, dear."

Even Alice Nicholas began to rub Frances the wrong

way. Alice was the dearest friend she'd ever had. She used
to say to her children: "There are all my friends, and then
there's Alice." People thought of her and Alice together,
and it was said that they even looked alike. Both were tall,
and on the skinny side, and both had premature gray
hair and large eyes, Alice's a greenish yellow, Frances's pale
blue. But whereas Frances tended to move a bit jerkily,
Alice had the grace of the natural athlete. Frances thought
she had never seen anything more charming than Alice and
Ted Nicholas waltzing together on the ice. But the greater
contrast was in their husbands. They had married polar
opposites: Frances, a self-made and compulsively hard-
working man; Alice, a charming idler, a president of mens'
clubs. Yet Ted and Stuart had always been the greatest
friends, perhaps for the very reason that they had never
competed.

Alice was an indefatigable shopper, and she would work
as hard helping Frances as when seeking an item for herself.
She decided that now was a good time for Frances to get
new curtains for the library in Bedford, and they went into
New York for the day. By noon they had been to six shops,
and Frances was exhausted. She slapped a hand on a maroon
material.

"This will do. I have to choose something."

Alice's lips were closed in a willful line. She was repress-
ing a criticism, out of respect for her friend's loss, but her
long gaze at the material, her slow head shake, were firmly
rejecting.

"Lunch," she said. "It's time for lunch."

"I want the maroon."

"Because you're tired and hungry, dear, is no reason to
take it out on your poor library."

They went to the Carlisle Club. Alice and Frances must

have lunched there a thousand times in the past three decades. Alice, as usual, ordered dry sherry for both.

"Of course, I know you don't give a damn about curtains," she said mildly. "You don't give a damn about anything yet. How could you?"

"But I do give a damn about lots of things. Perhaps not about curtains. I never did, really."

"Then you certainly put on a very good show."

"It was all for Stuart. And the girls. Now I live alone. I don't have to any more. Don't you see?"

When Alice's voice was soft, it could be very soft. "Of course I see."

Frances found herself staring almost sullenly at Alice's bracelet. It was heavy and jangling, made up of small gold golf clubs with rubies and diamonds at the ends. Ted had given her one for each of his championships. Alice wore no other jewelry, as if to balance this one seeming excess.

"Do you ever think perhaps we've given up too much for our husbands?" Frances asked. She took in how well her friend knew her from the latter's failure to register surprise.

"Perhaps. But we've enjoyed it."

"That may be just the trouble. Certainly neither your Ted nor my Stuart demanded it. I'm not blaming them. Women who turn themselves into carpets must expect to be trod on."

"I don't consider myself a carpet." There was the faintest note of pique in Alice's tone.

"Oh, I know you're an exquisite Aubusson! Or a Turkish masterpiece. Not like me, a poor old bath mat. But my principle is still there. You could have been a great decorator . . . or maybe the editor of *Vogue*." Alice laughed, with a touch of condescension. Were such things, colors and clothes and cosmetics, "real" things, like guns and sports and fishing prints and the sound of men's laughter from locker rooms?

"All right, skip *Vogue*," Frances continued impatiently. "Skip fashion. You could have been a teacher or a writer. You used to write very good things at school."

"Frances, pooh to you."

"But it's true! You have deliberately held yourself back, for Ted's sake. Or for what you thought was Ted's sake."

"I've had a very happy life, dear. Is that wrong? Is that selfish?" Alice paused. Frances knew that she was trying now to consider, although not very hard perhaps, that she might have been wrong. "Perhaps it *is* selfish to be as happy as I've been."

Frances knew that she should stop right there, but that she wasn't going to. "It's not only the career you've given up. I suppose you never really wanted one. It's the personality. You've never allowed yourself to be a woman who might make Ted the least bit uncomfortable."

"I should hope not!" Alice exclaimed proudly.

"Oh, I don't mean a scold or a crosspatch. You could never have been anything but lovely. I mean you've never let yourself become . . . well, an intellectual."

"If you mean I haven't turned myself into a bluestocking — thank you!"

At this Frances did pull herself together and dropped the subject. Just because she was beginning to have new doubts and misgivings was no reason to intrude on Alice's serenity. Alice might be as lost as she was if Ted should die, but then mightn't Alice have the luck to die first? She had always been lucky.

· · ·

Frances found that one did not have to be a widow very long before opportunities presented themselves for a change in one's social group. People who had not been particularly congenial with, or who had been awed by, her husband, would turn up to see if she might "do" in the next lap of life. Such a person was Josephine Stagg. She and Frances had been at Miss Dixon's Classes together, and she had had rather a crush on Frances, which had struck the latter at the time as something ominous and to be avoided. After school Josephine had married too often, usually in Europe, and had had a bout with morphine. Once, after a gap of several years, when Frances had run into her, rather too made-up, in the Carlisle Club, she had murmured in a husky voice: "Hi, Franny! Don't you recognize your old adorer? I've been to the dogs, but I'm back now." She was, too. She had proceeded to establish herself as one of New York's leading decorators.

Stagg had been her maiden name; she resumed it as the door slammed on minor German and Italian titles. Single, fat, loud and gorgeous she entertained the world of fashion in an old brownstone that she had made a blaze of color and flowers. When she and Frances met again at the Carlisle after Stuart's death, she asked her to dinner, and Frances murmured something about mourning. Josephine said there would be only three or four friends, and Frances accepted. When she arrived she found twenty. Josephine offered no apology, and Frances made no comment.

At dinner Frances found herself next to Manners Mabon, a very odd but very ebullient person. He told her that he was a bachelor, aged fifty-seven, and that he didn't have a job or a worry in the world. He was very stout and short, with a round, reddish face, white hair parted in the middle

and a high, affected voice that could be surprisingly author-
itative when he was not screeching with laughter at his
own jokes. People called him "Manny" and obviously regarded him as an authority on parties and gossip. Frances
couldn't help reflecting that Stuart would not have liked
him. But then he wouldn't have liked Josephine, either.

"And what do you do?" Frances asked him, when conversation at the table had fallen into pairs.

"Do, my dear lady? Why, bless you, I don't *do* anything. I live."

"But don't you have to do something besides live?"

"Why? I have eight thousand a year. It's not much, I
grant you. In fact, I believe it's near poverty in your
circles, but I have a darling old aunt who allows me to curl
up like a cat in a corner of her apartment. And then I eke
out the rest at the bridge table. I'm like the duchess in *The
Gondoliers*: 'At middle class party I play at écarté — and
I'm by no means a beginner.'" He arched his eyebrows to
underline his proficiency.

Frances was rather shocked by his financial candor, but
she was impressed, in spite of herself, that anyone could be
so confident on so little. She thought of all the guards that
she and Stuart had placed between themselves and this
man's impecunious state: the trusts, the insurance, the pen-
sion, the tax-free bonds. It would take a world disaster to
put them in Mr. Mabon's shoes.

"Have you never worked?"

"Oh, yes, from time to time. Actually, I had a job at St.
Christopher's School a couple of years back. One of the
teachers died, poor fellow, and the headmaster begged me
to fill out his term."

"But you didn't want to go on after that?"

"No."

"You didn't like it?"

"I didn't like the headmaster. He was intense, sincere, perhaps well meaning. But . . ." He paused, with an air of put-on gravity.

"But what?"

"He used the adverb 'hopefully' in sentences where it failed to qualify a verb, an adjective, or even another adverb."

Frances stared. "Was that all?"

"No. Worse is to come. Where you and I might have employed the expression 'best estimate,' he would say 'best guesstimate'! I am sorry to pain you, Mrs. Hamill, but he really did."

Frances was beginning to enjoy herself. "I hope there's no more to come."

"But there is. Once, just before I tendered my resignation, he suggested a joint session of the eighth and ninth grades for a discussion of the drug problem."

"And you disapproved?"

"Not of the idea. But of his proposition that we might thus obtain a 'cross-fertilization of ideas.' "

Frances nodded. "My husband hated that sort of thing, too. He used to call it jargon. He said it was a disguise for mental apathy."

Mr. Mabon accepted her switch of emphasis. He had not become a regular diner-out without learning his business. "Of course, he did. Your husband was a great man. But it must be depressing for you to be told that all the time. It must make you feel like a monument."

"Oh, you see that?"

"Everyone pushes you back in the past. Which doesn't

exist, really. I mean for living. We have only the present. And a little future."

"When you have four grandchildren, as I do, Mr. Mabon, you have to live a lot in the future. You want to make sure, anyway, that they have one. There are schools to think about, and colleges, and graduate schools —"

"But you must have plenty of money for all that!"

Frances made a little face at this. Her world was almost superstitious in its dread of ever suggesting there might be enough money for the future. "If I can keep ahead of inflation."

"Anyway, you can't live for grandchildren. Has it never struck you that a grandchild is actually a rather distant relation? He has only a quarter of your blood, like a second cousin."

Frances decided not to be irritated. He was too ridiculous. "It's easy to see you're not a family man. Why, I adore my grandchildren. Of course I can live for them. What do *you* live for?"

"Myself."

"But that sounds so selfish."

"It *is* selfish. I cultivate each minute. I am enjoying this soufflé. This fine white wine. I train myself not to think ahead even as far as dessert. Most people waste their lives anticipating the pleasures of the immediate future. But I am determined not to waste any present pleasure. I am determined, for example, not to waste the pleasure right now of talking with you."

"Thank you! It's a pleasure for me, too. But can we really live just like that? Mustn't we be doing things for other people?"

"Heaven forbid!"

"I mean in order to be happy. You can't be happy just living for yourself."

"Is there any other way? And I'm not at all sure it's not the only thing you *can* do for other people."

After dinner, in the drawing room, before the gentlemen joined the ladies, Frances asked Josephine about him. She replied that he was a darling and that she adored him.

"He tells me that he lives only for pleasure," Frances observed.

"That's all right if he gets it. So few people do."

"But doesn't it make him a terrible egotist?"

"It makes him a saint! Because the things that give him pleasure are the kindest, goodest things. Manny is always at some hospital or nursing home visiting some poor derelict whom everyone else has forgotten about. Why, he goes to see Mary Landon twice a week, and she's nothing but a vegetable. I doubt she even knows he's been there."

"Why does he go then?"

"Because he says it's just possible she might."

The men appeared now, and Manny smiled at Frances across the room.

"I suppose he's a . . ." She paused.

"A fag? Presumably. Unless he's too fat. Do you care?"

"Oh, no." And for a moment Frances persuaded herself that she actually didn't. The atmosphere at Josephine's was contagious.

Her new friend was too polite a guest to talk after dinner to his table companion, but when Frances left he insisted on walking her back to the Carlisle Club, where she was spending the night, though it was only a block away. He suggested that they visit an art gallery the next day to see the work of a young painter whom he admired, and she found herself agreeing without the slightest hesitation. And so her new relationship began.

He was nothing if not companionable. He seemed to have a genius for amusing himself and others. He talked a great deal, he almost bubbled, and showed a wide knowledge of art, literature and music, a shrewd eye and a keen ear. And yet Frances never had to interrupt him. He seemed to sense exactly when she wanted to speak, and he would listen as intently as he talked. Furthermore, he never seemed to be in a bad humor; he was always smiling, when he was not shouting with laughter. Occasionally he lost his temper, at a rude taxi driver or waiter, and then he could become quite commanding in this manner, but the mood quickly passed, and he would often apologize.

"Aren't you ever in the dumps?" she asked him once.

"Oh, my, yes. I have *abysses*. But then I hide. I won't be seen."

What did he see in *her*? Of course, she paid, at restaurants, at theatres, at exhibitions, but there must have been plenty of rich, lonely widows who would have been glad to pay for his company. And then, too, she was a bad bridge player and knew little about pictures and sculpture. Yet she had a strange sense that she was special to him. Was she a kind of older sister? A surrogate mother?

She found that she was spending more nights at the Carlisle Club instead of driving back to Bedford. She had given up the apartment in town when Stuart died as a needless expense; now she began to think of taking another small one. But in some ways she preferred the club. The anonymity of a rented bedroom pleased her. It committed her to nothing. When she closed her door, she closed out the world, even the consoling buzz of female chatter from the common rooms below. She had never sympathized with the point of view that condemns the even occasional segregation of the sexes. What she loved now about the Carlisle Club was that so much of life was suspended within its chaste Georgian walls: there was no sex, no home, no work, no duties. Was she getting as irresponsible as Manny himself?

"I think I begin to see what interests you in me," she suggested to him at last. "I'm a kind of tabula rasa. You see in me the perfect specimen of the philistine who denies her philistinism. Who defiantly affirms she's modern once she's paid her tribute to the accepted bourgeois ultima Thules. Picasso in art. Eliot and Pound in literature. Stravinsky in music."

"Let's put it that you interest me less because you are that, than because you see it. And seeing it, you can't really be it."

There seemed no limit to his eclecticism. If people incurred his scorn, no art did. He took her to a minimalist show at the Whitney and to an exhibit of Bouguereaus; he wept through *La Traviata* and listened with rapture to concerts in which she could detect nothing but dissonance and cacaphony; he urged her to read *Henry Esmond* and Nathalie Sarraute.

"But mightn't I lose all discrimination this way?" she asked him after they had attended a show of nineteenth-century sculptors of the Roman school. "Do I want to reach the point where I equate that nude Christian slave girl with the Venus de Milo?"

"Must we always be comparing things? There's only one great dividing line that we must never forget: between art that is serious and art that is not. But forgive me. There can be no such thing as art that is not serious. Between art and . . . well, what is not art."

"You judge, then, solely by the intention of the artist?"

"Not at all. I simply respect his intention. If it be serious."

She began to find it exhilarating to live in a world where no doors were banged shut. And she began as well to develop a pleasant and warming confidence that she was more to him than a promising pupil. She was coming to understand that he was a person incapable of subterfuge. The frank and open friendship that he offered meant as much to him as to her.

"I felt from the beginning that we might be friends," he told her. "I had a funny sense that your barriers were like those Indian bead curtains, easily thrust aside. And perhaps only put there to be thrust aside. You and I have both lived in worlds where communication is not much trusted. Yours has been one of reticences where clichés take the place of confidences. Mine has been one of garrulousness where too much candor creates the same blockage."

"Oh, it's true, Manny! I feel so easy with you."

"That's because we're learning to love each other. Oh, if you could see your eyes right now! My dear, you're horrified. But of course, I'm using that dirty old word in its Christian sense. Is that better? Can you relax now?"

"Isn't it funny?" she responded with a nervous titter. "Even in its Christian sense it still seems dirty to me. Or at least in poor taste, which is worse."

"Ah, but the fact you can say that shows how far you've come!"

"But how far am I going?"

"You see? You're still apprehensive. Love, you suspect, may land you in some very odd places. But don't worry, my dear. It commits you to nothing. You don't have to go anywhere. You're already there!"

"Where?"

"Having a little fun with poor old Manny. Is that so wicked?"

"I wonder if it isn't."

She was very nervous when he came out for his first weekend at Bedford. Leslie and Polly both had houses on the estate and would expect to be asked for a meal to meet any house guest of their mother's. And then there was Alice Nicholas, who had still not met him. Frances was not at all sure that it was wise to mix her new life with her old, but she had to do something about it. Leslie had already questioned her rather archly about Manny, and Alice's total silence had perhaps been more ominous.

He came out from the city by train on Saturday morning and was very enthusiastic about everything. Frances tried to imagine Crossways as it must strike him. It was a large, square, white old frame house, built more than a hundred years ago, to which had been added a modern wing with a living room, greenhouse and a pavilion over a swimming pool. It was a blend of the genteel old Westchester County with the prosperous new one; it was comfortable and homey and occasionally unexpected. It had oddly small rooms between the big ones and narrow corridors that led one to a proliferation of small stairways and different landings. It was decorated with good, but not the best, early American, and with Stuart's rather cautious collection of prints and watercolors: Audubon's birds and animals, English hunting scenes, Georgian political cartoons, and, here and there, a fine oil. Frances noted that Manny at once picked out the Martin Heade with the hummingbird and orchid. It was a man's house, she thought, a bit ruefully. One felt the touch of the late Stuart Hamill, the large-minded lawyer who was not going to allow any corner of his life to lack some grace.

"How do you run it all?" Manny wanted to know. "Can you get help out here?"

"I have a couple. And a part-time gardener."

"A couple!" he exclaimed with a laugh. "That's the height of sybaritism today."

Leslie had invited herself to lunch. It was warm enough to sit outside and the three had drinks on the terrace. Leslie was at her worst: bright-eyed, fidgety, insinuating, determined to be daring.

"Mummy tells me that you and she have been living the life of Riley, Mr. Mabon! I must say, I'm very envious."

Frances could feel that Manny was never going to like Leslie. She saw her daughter now through his eyes. Leslie too evidently considered herself the one sound member of a giddy clan. Her auburn hair had been rigidly set, probably just for this lunch; her puffy lips were ruby red. She had a way of tilting her head back as she talked, so that her gray-green, rather staring eyes could take in her interlocutor as someone to smile at, perhaps to condescend to. There was an air of self-obsession in her frozen combination of grin and grimace. It was as if she were constantly thinking: how do I look, how do I sound?

"I should have thought the term 'Riley' a bit florid to describe a respectable widow's existence," Manny retorted mildly.

"Oh, I think there's a great deal to be said for a widow's

life these days. Ma can travel and go to the theatre and tour the art galleries. In fact, she can do anything she jolly well wants to do. Unlike me, she doesn't have three great gangling girls at home, and a hungry husband to feed at night."

Frances reflected how little this description seemed to fit Leslie's ordered life in the small, perfect French house built on the best corner of the family property.

"But I don't suppose you'd change with her," Manny observed.

"I wouldn't change, no, Mr. Mabon," Leslie replied in a faintly reproving tone. "I adore my family, of course. All things in due time. What I mean is that it's good to be a wife and good to be a mother and — who knows? — it may be good to be a widow."

"That doesn't seem to be generally felt."

"It's certainly not generally *said*. But I had the distinct feeling, when my husband's father died, that my mother-in-law, deep down — oh, ever so far down, quite unconsciously, of course — may have had the tiniest feeling that she was now free to catch up with her friends on their garden tours and world cruises. They had been romping, so to speak, while she'd been tied to an invalid's wheelchair!"

"Your father was never an invalid, Leslie," Frances pointed out.

"Oh, Mummy darling, don't take things so personally. I wasn't suggesting that you're like my mother-in-law." She turned back to Manny. "But, still, the worst of it is over now, and Mummy's hardly an old woman. She can see whom she likes. She can go out with attractive men like you. Nobody could have a more trusting husband than my Felix, but I assure you that I would have quite a scene on my hands if I went gadding about the town like Ma!"

" 'Gadding,' " Manny mused. "It seems to me that the term rather deprecates your mother's activities."

"Oh, come now, Mr. Mabon. You do take one up on things. I simply meant that Mummy can now live for pleasure."

"It intrigues me how often wives seem to equate pleasure with the unmarried state."

"Evidently *you* do, Mr. Mabon."

"You mean because I've kept the best years of my life for myself?"

"Precisely."

Manny had a somewhat easier time with Polly, who came for tea in the afternoon, but even this was tense. If Polly believed, as Frances surmised (in what Polly would surely have deemed her mother's old-fashioned way) that women ought to have men's jobs, would Polly not also hold that at least some men should have women's, and did Manny justify his existence even as a children's nurse or housekeeper?

"I was hoping, Mr. Mabon, that you could get Mummy interested in some kind of work."

"Such as?"

"Well, would it really matter? Something where she'd be using her undoubted talents for a benefit to her fellow mortals."

"Do you think she should become a lawyer, like her brilliant daughter?"

Polly looked startled, though whether at his familiarity or at the oddness of his suggestion, Frances could not be sure. "But Mummy hasn't even a college degree. I'm afraid that particular form of social utility is out of the question."

"Has it ever occurred to you, my dear Polly, that your mother may be at least as useful to the profession of law as yourself?"

"No. How?"

"By being a client. Isn't she a client of yours?"

"Indeed she is. But how does that make her useful to the law?"

"By being useful to the lawyers. And isn't it true that the more mixed up a client's affairs are, the more the lawyer has to do? So that your mother can help you simply by creating problems for you to solve? The client and attorney — aren't they one and the same? Of equal merit?"

"But that's ridiculous! You might as well say that a great dentist is no more to be esteemed than his patient's sore tooth!"

"And so I do."

Polly was frankly exasperated. "Is there anyone you *do* admire, Mr. Mabon?"

"Certainly. The man or woman who creates beautiful things."

"And what of the people who admire those beautiful things?" Polly demanded with a note of triumph. "Aren't they as necessary to the artist as the sore tooth to the dentist? Shouldn't they be rated as highly?"

"But I'd never dream of denying it!"

Frances took Manny to church on Sunday morning. St. John's Chapel seemed the very definition of the term "Wasp." It was a clean, crisp, light, vaguely Palladian structure of yellow brick with big oblong windows showing, instead of biblical scenes in stained glass, the glory of the Westchester autumn woods. The congregation, in white pews enclosed by little doors, seemed of a spotless gray and white, in hair, in skin, in clothing; they raised mild voices to sing familiar hymns, holding hymnals at which they glanced only for the fourth or fifth stanza.

If there was something a bit dry in the air, a hint of the faded, of bygone fashion, of the survival of form and the evanescence of matter, Frances liked to believe that she could also make out something sweet, something fine and rare, as some old pressed leaf discovered in a gilded tome might suggest the deep, rich green of a primeval forest without the darkness, the danger, the lurking bandits, the sudden death. She liked to imagine that she was breathing the sanctified air of what was finest in a dead tradition: the simplicity, the probity, the reverence of Puritan forebears. Or was it just a congregation of ghosts?

She saw Alice Nicholas in the front of the church turn her head, but only for a second. Alice smiled and nodded at her, but no doubt her purpose had been to observe Manny. What would she make of him? What would any of them? Would a sociologist today find her friendship with Manny the symptom of a sterility that marked the last stages of a Wasp ruling class?

She liked the way Manny sang "There's a wideness in God's mercy," which preceded the sermon. He did not sing too heartily loud or too self-deprecatingly low; he did it as naturally as he talked and turned to her with a sly little smile of affected self-congratulation to point up the smugness of the lines:

"There'll be welcome for the sinner,
And more graces for the good."

The sermon was about death, how we must not refuse to think about it and talk about it. Manny seemed to take it all in, his eyes politely and sympathetically fixed on the minister as if the discourse were addressed exclusively to him. Frances was afraid of death; the prospects of extinction or eternity were equally appalling to her. She would try to tell herself that if there were an afterlife, there might be no time, but this was inconceivable. She shuddered now and tried to think of the words of a prayer. Then she turned to read the memorial plaque beside the pew. Then she murmured to herself: "O God, O God, O God." She looked out the window at the sunlight on the grass and felt a bit better. It *was* a beautiful church, after all, and there *were* good and kind people in it. Even if life in half the world was vile and miserable, this was still true. It was still part of the rest.

"And then you can't get away from death," the minister was saying. "We all think about it a good deal more than we care to admit — even to ourselves."

It occurred to Frances that her attitude towards religion was the rankest heresy, that she treated the hymns, the liturgy, the sermons, the flowers on the altar and the anthems of the choir, the very church itself, so fresh and varnished and white, so pure, as parts of an anesthetic to keep her free from the panic of the interstellar darkness. It wasn't that the Christian doctrine had to be true; it had simply to get her through. She wanted to live in distraction and die in her sleep.

She made herself think now of Stuart. She always felt guilty when she had not been thinking about him. It was as if, in living without considering him, she was depriving him of a portion of his afterlife. She thought of the great brow, the bushy eyebrows, the piercing eyes lit up with a constant laugh that denied the seeming total seriousness, the slow, soft, emphatic, lawyerlike tone, the constant little throat-clearings, the broad, round, continually shrugging shoulders, the heavy tweeded frame, the big arms and long, thin legs down to the old, well-polished shoes of finest leather. Was he laughing at her? Or frowning? Did he love her still? Or did he just pity her? Hadn't most of his love been an engulfing pity?

"Oh, Stuart, I miss you so!" she whispered.

It was a relief to think that if he were seeing her now, he must be seeing all of her. He would understand Manny; he would see him as a kind of friendly priest. A "priest," yes, that was the word! Was it? Almost at once she seemed to hear Stuart's braying laugh and see him joyously flinging an arm over Manny's shoulder, overwhelming him with benignity, playing with him, a big, genial cat, until the poor staring mouse was torn between gratitude at not being eaten and concern that he had been.

"Leave me Manny, Stuart," she silently prayed. "You had everything else."

After the service she drove Manny to Alice Nicholas's for Sunday lunch. Although she was not at all easy in her mind as to what they would make of each other, she knew what he would think of the house. It was a jewel, a long, low, pink Jacobean structure, partially ivy-covered, surrounded by a rich green lawn with elms and plots of rose-bushes planted right by the walls. The interior was surprisingly light; there was more glass than in the usual Jacobean house. In the living room a huge bay window rose two stories, and sunshine was dazzling on the heavy silver on the black mahogany tables and on the crimson covering of the chairs and sofa. Alice had chosen her period because it evoked a man's world, a huntsman's world, yet at the same time it offered the opportunity for an exquisite taste to operate, so to speak, under cover. In this way Alice would not "intrude" upon her husband.

There were some dozen guests at Alice's, including Frances's daughter Leslie. Ted Nicholas, big and bronze and handsome, a miracle at seventy, tweeded and broadly smiling, the kindest man in the world, immediately took Manny by the arm and introduced him around. Alice seemed unusually benevolent; they had obviously agreed to feature the new guest. Frances stood with Leslie a bit to the side.

"He seems so at home, your friend," Leslie observed.

Frances knew when Leslie was preparing to make a disagreeable remark. She had an air of suspended animation; her half-smiling, half-frightened eyes looked one up and down as if assessing one's probabilities of defense. She would probably be actually suffering, like a cow with distended udders, in her need to be relieved of whatever it was that she had in mind.

But Frances was not going to help Leslie. She simply looked at her.

"You know what they're saying, don't you?" Leslie continued.

"How can I, dear? Till you tell me."

Leslie's laugh was forced, hollow. "That you're the last person they ever expected to turn into a fag hag!"

Frances was so shocked that she almost showed it. "Really? I never dreamed I could become anything so fashionable."

"Oh, Ma, you're angry. Can't you take a joke?"

"No, Leslie, I can't. If I could, you wouldn't joke."

And she walked away. Of course, now there would be tears and telephone calls, and in the end it would be Frances who would have to apologize, but for the moment she didn't care.

She talked to Ted Nicholas, but she did not hear what he was saying. Fortunately, that rarely mattered with Ted. He was a kind of Parsifal, absurdly brave, absurdly good, absurdly naive. Stuart had once said that he was the only man he had ever known who was popular with other men and yet whose presence even in a locker room forestalled the dirty joke. His masculinity was too pure. But when he began to talk about Manny, she did listen.

"I like your little friend, Frances. Seems like a most cheerful guy. Nice to have around, I should think. Does he play golf, do you think? No? Would he like a lesson? I'd be very happy to give him one. Alice says he doesn't work. Well, neither do I! I never did, except once. Did I ever tell you? When I got out of Harvard my old man said I ought to do something, so I went to work for a bank. Well, I discovered my salary was exactly what I gave my chauffeur! They paid me on Friday, and I paid him on Saturday, so all I had to do was endorse the check. And then it dawned on me that if I didn't want to work, all I had to do was give up a chauffeur. So I've driven myself ever since!"

Frances had heard the story a dozen times before, but she usually liked it. Now, however, it was spoiled by his reference to Alice's remark about Manny's not working. Were they *all* against him? She shivered with sudden resentment. Could she not have *one* friend?

After lunch Alice, with her usual good manners, arranged for Manny to have a rubber of bridge. When two tables had been made up, and Ted had taken a friend on a tour of the kennels, she and Frances were free to stroll in the garden. Frances went straight to the point.

"You don't like Manny."

"Certainly I like Manny. I think he's entirely amiable."

"Then you don't like my friendship with him."

"You don't think it's a bit intense . . . a bit sudden?"

"What's wrong with that?"

"It's how it looks, Frances."

"Looks? Why should I care about looks?"

"I thought we both did. I thought it was important how we appeared to the world. As our husbands' wives. As our children's mothers. It's not that what's inside isn't more important. Of course it is. But I thought you and I believed that our outward selves should reflect, as far as possible, the things we stand for."

"And how does Manny's being my house guest affect that?"

"It's not just his being your house guest. It's your being with him so constantly. Being seen giggling together in art galleries —"

"Giggling? We may have been laughing."

"Giggling was the way it was put to me."

"Really, Alice, are you taking to gossip?"

"I have compelled myself to listen. For your sake. Do you want to know what people are saying about you?"

They were in the greenhouse now, before the glory of Alice's begonias. Alice used to say that the begonia was the ultimate flower. Frances trembled with dismay as she forced herself to admit that her friend's sincerity and good will were beyond dispute. She was as fine as her favorite flower. She had made a beautiful thing of Ted's life. Frances glanced at the bracelet of gold golf clubs.

"What do they say?" she asked miserably.

"Well, I don't have to be told that he calls you 'darling.' He must have done so a dozen times at lunch."

"But that just means 'you' in his world!"

"It's not a world that I admire."

"Are people going to say that he's my lover?"

"That would be flattering him. I doubt they wish to."

"Then what is the harm, really?"

"The harm, my dear, is what you do to yourself. The harm is in the picture of Stuart Hamill's widow giggling about New York, hand in hand with a silly, shabby, fat man who needs a free meal every time he's had an unlucky evening at the bridge table."

"Oh, Alice!"

"There, dear. I've said it. I shall not say it again. That Mr. Mabon is amiable and trustworthy I am happy to concede. But that's how it looks. Let me show you my black iris. It's the prize."

That evening, before supper at Crossways, Frances sat alone with Manny in the living room. She felt uncomfortable and constrained; it disturbed her that he should have picked that very moment to discuss his theory of friendship. There were friends, he told her, and "real" friends. Real friends had to have absolute trust in each other. Communication had to be always truthful, though reticence was permissible. He had had only two "real" friends in his life. She was the third. He was very grave about it, quite unlike his usual bubbling self. Perhaps this was why it took him so long to observe her distraction.

"Something has happened," he noted at last, after watching her fumble in her pocketbook for a cigarette. "Something has upset you."

"Oh, it's all too ridiculous."

"Not too ridiculous to have agitated you, darling."

"I wish you wouldn't call me that."

"Very well." She had expected that his eyes would show anger, but they didn't. He could be angry at people — oh, she had seen that! — but he wasn't now. "I'll try not to."

"Oh, Manny, I'm sorry." She reached for his hand and squeezed it. The only way she could bring up the subject was to pretend not to know. "What is a fag hag exactly?"

"Ah, that's it." He laughed in a hard, would-be cheerful manner. "A fag hag is an older woman, a society type, who surrounds herself with younger homosexuals. The typical fag hag would be a jeweled harridan with some blond kid in tow. Have people been calling you a fag hag?"

"Leslie says so."

"Leslie is spiteful, but she may be right. People will say anything. And how they hate friendship! Friendship somehow seems to threaten them. When they see any two human beings form such a relationship, they'll break their necks to give it some kind of a sexual slant. Does it bother you terribly to be called a fag hag? Because of me?"

"I suppose it does. And, anyway, you're not a —"

"A fag? No. I should be, but I'm not. It's ridiculous. I suppose I put on my weight to make myself unattractive. And protect me from it. My gay friends call me an honorary queer."

"I'm sorry, Manny. I know I started it but I find I hate this kind of talk."

"Well, let's put it on the table, once and for all, and then we can leave it. You can decide whether or not you want to go on being my friend. Truth is everything, darling — I mean Frances. You see? You should have told me you objected the very first time I used that term. Be frank. Shall I tell you now just how I came to be what I am? Whatever that is?"

She agreed, but she was still glad when the cocktails arrived. Manny told his story succinctly and well. It was a Boston boyhood, a Boston background, brave, frugal, high-minded, laden with disaster. There was the father, killed in the Ardennes in 1917, and the two older brothers, both athletes, drowned off Manchester in a sailing race. Manny, a posthumous child, had been left alone to comfort an old mother, who had borne him at forty and who had supported her family as headmistress of a fashionable girls' school.

"Mother was simply everything to me," he explained. "You can't imagine her kindness and courage, her simple greatness. I knew that I was all she had left, and we simply clung to each other. There was us, and there was the world. Even the girls at her school, even the teachers, were 'world.' Mother cared for them — she was a crackerjack of a headmistress, efficient, strong — but they had nothing to do with 'us,' the inner citadel. To me they were dangerous, and Ma protected me. The school was hung with big, dark prints of academic paintings of historical scenes. One had a particular fascination for me. It showed Catherine de' Medici, followed by her ladies, emerging from the Louvre to inspect the corpses of the St. Bartholomew's Day massacre. The foreground was littered with male bodies, some partially stripped. Only partially, mind you. It was an academic picture. The Queen Mother's ladies exhibited a variety of expressions: fright, horror, scorn, elation. Only Catherine was cold, contained, impassive."

"And how did you interpret that?"

"Well, the men were dead, and the women survived; that I must have noted. It was dangerous to be a man and perhaps an unholy thing to be a woman. There was safety only in the erect, black-garbed figure of the Queen Mother."

"But wasn't she responsible for the massacre? Wasn't she a fiend? Surely you didn't accuse your poor mother of *that*?"

"Who knows what my subconscious may have accused the poor creature of? All I knew, deep down, was that she was on my side. That with her was safety. That is how I feel about you, too. And so it was that when I went to boarding school and was tempted to do those things with other boys, the image of Mother always kept me from it. Fear kept me from the girls; fear, or respect of Mother kept me from the boys. At this point, ten years after Mother's death, I am not sure which had the greater, or the less, attraction. All I know is that I have always been a monk and will now remain one."

"But, Manny, what a tragic story!"

"It's not tragic at all. I've been a jolly monk. Millions of men and women have been celibates by choice. I have lived as fully as most of the people we know. As Alice Nicholas, for example."

For the first time she caught the note of antagonism in his tone. Manny was not quite as dispassionate as he liked to think. He despised Leslie, but he hated Alice. Frances sighed and closed her eyes. She was going to have to choose between her two friends. And it was bitter evidence of how frail a creature Stuart Hamill's God had made her that she was going to find that choice so hard a one.

"Pray for me, Manny," she said with a wry smile. "Pray for me . . ." She closed her eyes as she made the ultimate effort to bring out the detested word. "Darling."

The Reckoning

ROSA KINGSLAND was the same age as the century; she had just passed her sixtieth birthday when she received the final verdict from the Dunstan Sanatorium about her son.

"We are sorry to inform you that not only is there no immediate prospect of Meredith's being able to resume a normal life, but, in the opinion of at least one of our medical staff, it may be years before it will be advisable to release him from the institution. And we are afraid that we cannot advise your further visits while his resentment against his family and home is still so intense."

Rosa stared at the letter, wondering stonily if she were inhuman to see only a bill in its terms. But thirty thousand a year, that was what it added up to, not to mention the other fifteen just to keep her husband in his wheelchair on the floor above. At last slowly, ineluctably, the tears began to bubble up in her resisting eyes. Did tears matter? Did they make her any more absurd than she always had been: a stout Chinese Buddha with a round face and short gray curled hair? But a weeping Buddha — how ridiculous.

Calm again now — as calm and stolid as she usually managed to be — she rose and went to the wall to take down
The Betrothal, one of Gorky's earlier versions. What should
she put in its place? Why, what but what *had* been there,
forty-odd years before, in her grandmother's day, and
which was still presumably in the attic with the others of
the old lady's collection, its face to the wall, the very dearest of dear little Tuscan peasant girls, a pitcher balanced on
one shoulder, painted in Florence by Luther Terry in
1876. God.

She turned her reading lamp full on the Gorky and sadly
studied it. She knew about the "biomorphic" images drawn
from sexual organs, but she had suppressed them. It didn't
make any difference what she thought so long as she kept it
to herself.

What *she* saw in her Arshile Gorky . . . ah, that was what
made the difference. It was simply the most beautiful picture in the world — except for the *Resurrection* of Piero
della Francesca that she and Amory had seen at Borgo San
Sepolcro and which Aldous Huxley had called the greatest
painting ever painted, so that was that. But the Gorky, a
symphonic poem of light gray, dark gray and black, with
flashes of yellow and red and soothing traces of pale green,
evoked for her a fashionable ladies' store on Madison Avenue
with round glass-topped tables, lamps on tall steel poles,
elegant high-heeled slippers and the suggestion of beautiful
women, soft-skinned Circes, worldly-wise, corrupt, stony-
hearted. Yet broken up as they were into bits and pieces,
their menace was muted and their loveliness intensified. It
was always so in a world that concealed beauty behind every
horror if you could only pull it out. Her imagined ladies
made Rosa think of the answer of the Abbé Mugnier to a

leering anticleric who had surprised him admiring a painting of nudes bathing: *"C'est un état d'âme, monsieur!"*

She heard the sound of her husband's wheelchair in the corridor and looked up to see the wizened little man squinting at her from the doorway. His eye took in the painting on the floor.

"Poor Rosa," he cackled. "Must that go, too?"

"What else?"

"You could put Merry in a state institution, you know. I would, if I were you."

She noted his "you." Meredith was hers now. This was his way of recognizing that his money had been spent and that they lived on what was left of hers. Oh, yes, it was all hers, for whatever good it might do her, the shabby narrow red brick house with the high Dutch gable on Tenth Street that she had inherited from her grandmother, with the late Victorian horrors for which the old lady had unwisely exchanged her Federal treasures; the dwindling pile of securities at the United States Trust Company; Amory, his wheelchair and senile complaints; and Meredith, dreadful Meredith, at Dunstan. And her pictures. Soon enough, no doubt, to be only a picture. She shuddered at the thought of the Max Ernst downstairs in the tiny gallery that had once been the maids' dining room.

"He'll eat us out of house and home, that's what he'll do," Amory continued petulantly.

"Not so long as I have anything left to sell."

"And how long will that be?"

"A year, maybe."

"I must admit that your crazy things have brought more than any rational man could have guessed. Do you suppose you're selling them too soon?"

"Oh, much too soon! But I didn't buy them to make money."

"And what will you do when the year is out? Though I don't suppose it'll be my problem. I shan't be around much longer." If his pause was to give her the opportunity to contradict his prognostication, it was in vain. "I suppose you can sell this house for a bundle. You won't need more than a couple of rooms then."

"I shall need the house when Meredith comes home."

"And when will that be?"

"When the last picture has been sold."

"Because he'll know there's no more money for his shrinks?"

"No. Because he'll have been cured."

The most shattering discoveries can come very quietly, perhaps because they are not really discoveries. One has suspected them all along. Rosa helped her husband's nurse to push his chair into the tiny elevator where it just fitted. The nurse closed the door and then descended the narrow stairway to the front hall to meet him and take him for his morning circumnavigation of the block. Rosa, alone in the house, sat on the sofa before the empty grate and allowed the pallid ghosts of her early years to possess her.

She remembered the day when she had told her grandmother about Amory. The old lady had been sitting by the fire in the black silk that she always wore, inattentively nodding that handsome head with the fine Greek profile and high-piled, beautifully set white hair. Her head was like a fine piece of sculpture on a black ball; it moved around on top of a motionless body like an owl's. In her childhood Rosa had used to wonder if she could turn it around entirely and look backwards.

"I'm engaged to Amory Kingsland, Grandma."

"What are you telling me, child? Amory Kingsland? Are you sure you understood him correctly?"

"Quite sure. He was very plain. And anyway, what else could he have meant?"

"What will you live on? I hope he's not counting on me."

"Oh, no, Grandma. He says he can support me. We shan't need a great amount."

Perhaps some memory of her dead son, alcoholic and bankrupt, and of her dead daughter-in-law, victim of an overdose, flickered in the mind of the grandparent. Perhaps even something like remorse. "Well, you'll have what I have when I'm gone, child. It'll be something."

"Oh, Grandma, don't even think of that!"

"I'm sure Amory thinks of it." The old lady snorted. "He must be your senior by twenty years."

"Only fifteen."

"Think of it. Amory Kingsland. Well, I suppose it's better than being the last leaf on the tree."

Rosa thought that it was a good deal better. She knew that tree. It was true that Amory was a fussy, dyspeptic, excitable little man, sputtering with ideas and theories that nobody listened to, and that he had a mincing manner, round soft cheeks and short hair, brushed close to his scalp and parted in the middle, that looked like a wig. And he was always the first on his feet at a banquet to offer a fulsome toast or tribute. But he was harmless and kind, and she fancied that he would not be difficult to live with. He had no job, but he belonged to enough clubs and patriotic societies to ensure his being out of the house a good part of the day.

What was the word for it — symbiosis? If she needed to get away from Granny, he needed a wife to make him look like other men. He was no more attractive to women than she to men. To find a mate, other than each other, they would have had to fish in lower social pools. And she had been right. It had worked.

The only times in the early years that she had found herself impatient with Amory was in their trips to Europe. He fancied himself a connoisseur of the arts and loved to quote John Addington Symonds on the Italian Renaissance. At home Rosa had trained herself not to hear him except for certain phrases that gave her a cue for rejoinders such as: "Really, dear?" or "Amory, you *are* extraordinary," but when they were actually in the presence of a masterpiece she found him tediously distracting. Pictures had always stirred a chord within her that was unlike any other vibration, and she hated to be talked to while viewing one.

On a visit to the Sistine Chapel in the hot summer of 1938 his chatter became suddenly intolerable. He was hopping briskly about, pointing upwards to illustrate the "tactile values."

"But all those terms came later. This was a church, Amory. People came here to worship."

He tittered at her insularity. "Really, Rosa, do you think Michelangelo believed all that rubbish? He only painted religious subjects because the pope made him."

"Exactly. He didn't believe in anything. One doesn't have to believe in anything."

Amory blinked at her. "And just what, pray, do you mean by that extraordinary statement?"

"I don't know what I mean. And I don't care."

"Maybe the heat's too much for you, my dear. We'd better go back to the hotel."

"I'm going to sit right here. Let me be, please, Amory. For half an hour, anyway. Go look at the Raphael portrait of Leo X. That's your favorite, isn't it?"

The next day, in a modern gallery, she bought her first painting. It was a lyrical abstraction called *Hills and Ocean*, a study in pallid, fragile blues and pinks and darker greens, done with thin paint. It made Rosa think of a summer trip that she had taken as a child with her father to Mount Desert Island in Maine.

"Bar Harbor?" Amory inquired with a snort when she showed it to him at the hotel. "It looks more like an old rag the artist used to rub his hands with. May I ask what you paid for it?"

"Two hundred and fifty dollars."

"My God, woman, are you out of your mind?"

But he thought she was even more so the next day when she received a polite note from the artist, a young American, asking her to come to a party at his studio. She informed Amory that she planned to accept.

"But we don't even know him!"

"We will when we get there. He's very pleased at my purchase and would like me to see some of his other things."

"How did he get your name?" Amory demanded suspiciously.

"From the gallery, of course. You don't have to go. I'm perfectly all right by myself."

"In Rome? With a crowd of artists? All Fascists, or maybe even Communists? Of course, I'll have to be with you."

"That's up to you. But in any event I'm going."

The studio was six flights up, on the top of an old house, and Amory protested bitterly at almost every step. They were greeted at the door by the young artist, George, who was small and dark and charming and made Rosa think of Little Billee in *Trilby*. When he handed her a drink and took her to a window to overlook the busy rooftops of the neighborhood, she had a moment of intense pleasure and almost forgot about Amory. In a short time she was actually telling the nice young man what she fancied she could see in his painting. Was it the gin?

"But you must think my approach is hopelessly subjective and sentimental," she exclaimed ruefully.

But he was nice. "Not at all. It's always allowable to see something organic in my work. You should never be ashamed, anyway, of what you see in a picture. It is the creation, after all, of two persons."

"Wouldn't that mean it's not one but several things? Or as many as there are viewers?"

"Well, what's the harm in that? Anyway, I think your eye is a good one. It saw something good in me."

This was delightful, but his friends were bound to spoil it. One of them, a large, unshaven, hirsute man, spoke to her with a rather abrasive assurance.

"Don't believe George, Mrs. Kingsland. He's always trying to appease people he suspects of being antiabstractionists. He thinks, if he allows them their fantasies as to what his lines and squiggles represent, that they will buy his daubs. But some of us are made of sterner stuff. I'd be happy, ma'am, if you'd buy one of mine, but I'm not going to let you think I approve of your finding it 'organic.'"

"Well, I'm sure I shouldn't," Rosa said hastily. "And, of course, I'd love to see your things. What do you try to depict in them?"

"If I could tell you that, ma'am, I wouldn't have to paint them."

"Oh, I see."

The laughter of the little group seemed more mocking than friendly. One of the girls, who had long straight hair, bold eyes and a sacklike dress of dull brown, now asked her in a voice that seemed poised on the impertinent:

"Do many of your class back home still like pictures that tell a story?"

"My class?"

"You know. Society people."

Rosa decided that she had better not be offended. "Well, even if we liked them, where would we find such pictures?"

"She's got you there, Carol," the big man said to the brown dress in a tone that almost made Rosa think he was taking her side. "Those people have been frightened out of their natural tastes. We've browbeaten them into thinking if they dislike something, it must be good."

"Anyway, I don't care for pictures that tell stories," Rosa affirmed.

"Even if you make them up yourself?" the tall man asked with a laugh that was almost a sneer.

Rosa was wondering if she might not find the courage to take him on when she heard her husband's shrill voice across the room addressing another group:

"Well, say what you will, I'd take the Sargent gallery in the Tate for all the modern art on this planet!"

In the silence that followed this she knew that her plight was hopeless. Even if by some miracle of effort she was able to establish a thin line of communication between herself and these young people, Amory would be there to sever it. Never the twain would meet.

In the taxi returning to their hotel Amory rattled on against young "anarchists" and deplored her getting involved with them. She waited for an appropriate pause and then put in firmly:

"It's all right, Amory. You needn't worry. You will never have to go to a party like that again."

"You mean you'll go without me?"

"No, I shan't go either. It's not seemly. We don't belong there."

"Well, I should hope not! And while you're making good resolutions, how about promising me not to buy any more of their crazy pictures?"

"No."

"No?" He glanced at her quickly, surprised at the metallic quality of her tone. "You mean you're going to throw good money after bad? And get more of that junk?"

"Yes, I think I may, Amory."

"And do you expect me to finance this new craze?"

"You needn't. I have my own money now." Grandma had died the year before, having held out till ninety-six and spent most but not all of her principal.

Amory was used to directing even the minor events of their domestic routine, but he knew that on the rare occasions when, for reasons incomprehensible to him, she took a stand, she was unbudgeable. Indeed, she knew how to make him feel at such times that he did not exist as a force in her life. He could then only retreat into sulkiness.

"You'd better hope I don't go mad, too. You'd better pray that our joint exchequers don't founder in lunatic collecting."

"But I should love to see you collect, Amory. You might even find you had an eye for it."

In the decade that followed, Amory never altered his attitude of contemptuous disapproval, but he learned to confine his opposition to that. The years of the second world war were important ones to Rosa because she made friends with a gaunt and taciturn gallery owner near Washington Square who knew some of the painters who were refugees from France and Germany, and was able to introduce her to the school that became known as abstract expressionism. Silas Levine seemed to understand her intuitively; he never talked technically about pictures, but simply showed them to her. If she liked one, he would nod and show her another. He made her feel that if two people were lucky enough to share a discriminating taste, they had no need to discuss it.

"Come by next week, Mrs. Kingsland. I'll have some drawings of Adolph Gottlieb's that may amuse you."

But if Rosa had reduced her husband to at least a sullen acceptance of her acquisitions, she had no such success with her son. Meredith seemed to have inherited all of the conservative genes of his great-grandmother but little of her ability to cope with the world. When she hung a Miró sketch in his bedroom as a surprise, she found it face down on the floor in the hall the next day.

"At least let me have my own room to myself, Mummy!" he bawled at her. "You've got the whole rest of the house for your garbage!"

Everybody considered Meredith a hopeless problem but Meredith himself. His self-confidence seemed to grow with the checks that life put in his way until total failure was crowned with total arrogance. Tall, awkward, with shiny, long black hair, and spindly limbs, his big, staring pop eyes and high, harsh, jeering voice seemed to be calling down the world for its idiotic failure to appreciate Meredith Kingsland. He could never be sent away to camp, boarding school or even an out-of-town college. He was simply too fumbling to take proper care of himself, yet not enough of a freak to win exemption from the physical hostility of his peers. He went for twelve years to a mild, genteel boys' school on the east side of Central Park of which Amory was a trustee, and thereafter took endless courses in literature and history at City College.

Insofar as Meredith seemed able to take in the dismal lacks in his life — lack of a job, lack of a girl, lack of any body of friends — he blamed "Mummy" for them. She had cared too much and too little about him. She had fretted unduly over his health and then criticized him for playing no outdoor games. She had puffed his imagined virtues, making an ass of him in their social circle, and had then been hypercritical of any composition he produced. She embarrassed him by her heaviness and dowdiness and then criticized him for spending so much time and money on his own appearance.

Meredith's greatest ally was whoever happened at the moment to be his psychiatrist.

"Doctor Cranch thinks your real family are your pictures, Mummy. He says that's what's my basic trouble."

"Did he really say that, Meredith? Or did he suggest that one of your troubles might be that *you* thought it?"

"Don't you think I even know what my own doctor says?"

"I think you sometimes edit him for my benefit."

"Why should I want to do that?"

"To get even with me, dear. A son can't lose, can he? He takes full credit for his assets and blames Mummy for his liabilities."

"Really, Rosa," Amory intervened, "aren't you being a bit hard on the boy?"

"Oh, what does she *care*?" Meredith cried angrily. "What does she care for but her silly old art?"

Indeed, Rosa had to admit, after one of these meals, that all she *did* want was to get back to her silly old art. She liked nothing better than sitting alone in a room with her pictures, looking at them and thinking about the things they conjured up in her mind.

She understood that many observers of the art of Franz Kline found in his bold blacks and whites a sense of the violence and power of large, dark, coal-besmirched cities, and in the trajectories of hurtling black across passive white planes an image of encroachment and forcible possession. But what she chose to make out in her Kline was not a twisted mass of steel beams but a giant menacing insect, seen through a magnifying glass, whose only function was to destroy and consume its lesser fellows, and in this horned, multilegged monster she had no difficulty in identifying her late grandmother. Yet this interpretation gave her no pain or unease; on the contrary, it seemed to bind her father's parent into a web of beauty that she could accept and love.

Even more factitious was what she read into her Motherwell, one of his *Elegies to the Spanish Republic*. She had heard that Motherwell had not visited Spain until after the civil war, and she had taken this as her excuse to deviate from his title. Besides, were the titles of modern paintings not notoriously misleading? In the old academic days one had known just where one was. *Henry IV Barefoot in the Snow before the Gates of Canossa* meant just that. But did she have to identify the black pole-like figure and the two black spheres on either side as the phallus and testicles of a sacrificial bull nailed to a whitewashed wall? No. It was a beautiful evocation of the trunk of the old elm tree in the garden in Newport with the dumpy figures of her two maiden aunts, always in mourning, and the whole concept was death.

Little by little her pictures had begun to fill the house. Amory continued to grumble, but he didn't really care what she hung on the walls, and she put none in the dining room where the family conversations occurred. Meredith objected more vociferously, but she had given him a whole floor where he could surround himself to his heart's content with his great-grandmother's Turkish bazaars and Tuscan peasant girls. There were moments, however, when she had to remind him that it *was* her house. She dared not go further and suggest that he get his own apartment. Meredith, faced with the smallest threat of what he called "rejection," was likely to become hysterical.

The family friends and cousins, almost without exception, looked upon "Rosa's daubs" as a kind of harmless mania to which it was kinder not to draw too much attention. They could not be unaware of the growing importance of abstract art in the city around them, but they maintained their silent but united front against it, lumping it as one of the not-to-be escaped evils of a decadent society, along with high taxes, drugs, over-stressed civil rights and the bad manners and promiscuity of youth. Yet even in their ranks there was an occasional deserter, and Rosa sometimes found an adventurous individual arriving ahead of the other guests at one of her dinner parties to have a peek at the little gallery off the hall.

Silas Levine decided at last that she had gone far enough to justify him in seeking to penetrate her reserve.

"You know, Rosa, in any other social milieu but yours you'd be considered a remarkable woman. Why do you cling so to your constipated little group of antediluvians?"

"It's my husband's world. He hasn't any other."

"But don't you ever crave the company of people who care for the things you care about?"

"Then I can come to you."

He laughed and gave it up. "All right, Rosa. Maybe you're right. Maybe your pictures are enough."

Sometimes artists wished to see her collection, and she would make arrangements through Levine for them to come to the house at times when neither her husband nor son would be home. This became more difficult after Amory had his stroke and was permanently in the house, but the little hall gallery, discreetly used, still answered her purpose. Only if Meredith happened to be going in or out of the house at the time was the visitor likely to be startled by the shrill voice from the dark hall exclaiming: "Are you in there, Mummy? Who's being polite enough to look at your zany show?"

Meredith, in his late twenties, unoccupied except for his daily hour with his analyst, seemed to have nothing to do now but hound his mother. Family meals had become a torture to her.

"All I really want to find out, Mummy — seriously — is how to tell the difference between a good abstract and a bad one. It can't be by whether or not it resembles something, because it isn't anything, is it? And you can't say that a line or a curve is badly drawn, because the artist can always say that's the way he meant it. So what standard have you left to go by? What do you look for?"

"I guess I just look."

"Oh, Mummy, what kind of an answer is that? You have to look *for* something in a picture."

"Do you, Meredith? But, anyway, I think I *can* tell a bad abstract. There were some at the Junior League show."

"But how did you know?"

"By what they did to me. They gave me a dead feeling. I wanted to turn away. I wonder if that isn't the only way to teach art. Perhaps we make a mistake in dragging classes of children through museums' past masterpieces. It might be more effective to show them the discards in the cellar."

"So that's your only criterion: a kind of gut feeling?"

"I'm afraid so."

Amory, embittered by his stroke, tended to side with his son in these arguments, but not without getting in an occasional thrust at the latter. "Just as I suspected, the whole business is a kind of emotional pudding. But you ought to understand that, Meredith. Doesn't your shrink explain those things to you? Don't you suppose those dots and squiggles are sexual symbols to your poor frustrated mother? Why not? Married to an old man in a wheelchair she must dream of something better, mustn't she? Now don't get excited, Rosa, I'm blaming myself, not you. What can a poor, impotent creature like me . . ."

But Rosa had already left the table. In the silence of her own chamber she contemplated the serene truth of the parallel lines of her Mondrian and turned her mind firmly from humanity as represented in the dining room below. For once she was not subjective.

Not long after this conversation Meredith took too many sleeping pills and was revived only with difficulty. It was not clear that he had intended a fatal dose — he might have simply planned a melodrama — but his psychiatrist recommended commitment to the Dunstan Sanatorium, and once there, there seemed little possibility of any early release. Six years elapsed, and Rosa's collection, one by one, ascended the auction block. She thought of them as the pale, proud victims of a reign of terror, silently mounting the steps of the scaffold. She never wished to learn who had bought any of them.

When she went to Silas Levine's gallery to tell him that she would have to sell the Gorky, he threw his hands up in anger and disgust.

"You've said yourself, Rosa, that the whole thing is a kind of mad revenge on Meredith's part. Well, don't give in to it! Tell that monstrous minotaur of a sanatorium that it can no longer have its annual sacrifice. Your son will be no worse off at home than he is there. And you could at least keep the poor remnant of your glorious collection."

"But how can I be sure that Meredith, once out, won't try it again?"

"Well, you have to take some chances. What sort of a life does he have in that loony bin, anyway? Rosa, they're gobbling you up, eating you alive!"

"I see that, Silas. But what you don't see is that I've deserved it."

"Oh, my God, you Puritans! *How*, pray, have you deserved it?"

"Because I've given so little to my husband. And really nothing at all to poor Meredith."

"And what have they given you?"

"Nothing, it is true. But they had nothing to give."

"No love?"

"Some people have no love to give."

"Well, if they gave you nothing, and you gave them nothing — or very little, as you say — why aren't you square?"

"Because, you see, I did have something to give."

"Love?"

"Love."

"And what did you do with your love?"

"You, of all people should know that, Silas. I'm not complaining. I've had a good life. The time has come to pay for it, that's all."

Levine, staring at her, at last gave up, as he always had to, with Rosa. "Let me do one thing for you, anyway. Let me put together a beautiful album of colored photographs of every picture from your collection!"

She smiled as she shook her head. "Do you really think I need that, Silas?" There was a pause in which he made no answer. "Now tell me. What can I get for the Gorky?"

The "Fulfillment"
of Grace Eliot

THE QUIET, EVEN ROLL of my retirement days, like the swelling of a sluggish sea, has been rudely shattered by my discovery of Grace Eliot's love letters. They have erupted on the surface of my placid existence like a breaching whale, leaving a turmoil of tumbling white water which has threatened to drown me. It was not, of course, that the love affair of which they form the sole hard evidence was generally unsuspected. The name of the late great novelist has long been linked with that of Leonard Esher. But before the emergence of these letters no one but myself could have proved that Grace and he had been lovers. And I for thirty years have kept silent, believing as I did (and, despite everything, still do) that the affair had been uncharacteristic and basically unimportant, and that Grace, having recovered from a momentary lapse in taste and judgment, had been relieved to devote the balance of her life to her art with hardly a glance over her shoulder at a dead past.

As her literary agent (not to mention her disciple and worshiper) I had been entrusted by her husband with the custody of her papers and with the task of making these available — at my discretion — to biographers and students. I had had all the documents catalogued and was confident of my familiarity with them all, but there was a bundle of snapshots tied together by an elastic band that I had never considered worth examining. It was labeled "Dogs," for Grace, unlike myself, had been an ardent lover of canines. Last week, when I happened to move this package, seeking for something else in its drawer, the old band broke, and the photographs spilled out, exposing the five letters to Leonard Esher. Perhaps Grace had felt the doghouse to be an appropriate hiding place for her erstwhile pet! To me it was eminently fitting that he should have been kenneled with curs.

She had presumably asked him to return the letters when their affair had ended. Grace's breezy, complacent spouse, Andrew, who must have enjoyed a dozen adulteries to his wife's meager one, might not have cared if they were published or not, but Grace, even in the easygoing nineteen forties, had had an intense sense of privacy. Her standards had been high for all human relationships and the highest of all — as expressed in her novels — for love. The mere idea of a vulgar word, a knowing shove in the ribs, would have been to her the vilest desecration. It was in keeping with her character that no word should have been spoken of her indiscretion and no memorial kept.

But now I had painfully to revise my long enshrined opinion of this episode in her life. Not only was I faced with love letters; I was faced with passionate ones. It appalled me to find Grace, that high, proud soul who could hardly endure to sit in a room with an ugly chintz, whose garden had seemed an effort to redecorate the very landscape, a novelist whose jeweled allegorical tales were said to have rivaled Lafcadio Hearn's, wailing like a raw schoolgirl in this appalling prose:

> Oh, love of my life, imagine Brunhild, having lain for years in dreamless sleep, lulled by the crackle of the flames that Loge, at his sire's bidding, had kindled to protect her from the intrusion of any but the bravest warrior, awakening to the silver clarion of Siegfried's horn only to discover that she is . . . old!

The picture of Leonard as Siegfried is ludicrous enough, but the idea of Grace as old is even more so. In 1946 Grace, barely forty, was still a brilliant spectacle, tall and fair — what used to be admiringly called willowy — with rich golden hair, straight and shimmering, tied in a large knot at the nape of her neck, and the whitest skin, the bluest eyes, the most perfect features I ever saw. Leonard was older than she, at least ten years older, with gray hair and cold gray-blue eyes, so nattily dressed as to seem almost a parody of himself, and smiling, always smiling, as if smiles could protect him from the obvious charge of dilettantism. Leonard, in my uncharitable opinion, was too lazy and too egocentric to love anybody, too inert to bother himself with any but the pleasantest and most perfunctory news of his friends. It baffled me how Grace could have so admired this thin creature, even while seeing through him — for it was notorious that the shallow "villains" of her fiction were all modeled on Leonard. Was it a form of masochism?

Such, anyway, was the man who for a decade before their actual affair had seemed to dominate her life, always at her parties, always at her side, the intimate of her husband

as well as herself, a constant cool presence, giving off his
advice and opinions in the languid tone of one accustomed
to being listened to, judging everything and everybody,
sneering at the universe, at the Eliots, at himself. Oh, people buzzed, of course. Was it a triangle? A design for living? Nobody could be sure.

And now must I, the sole survivor, bring these letters to
public light and see Leonard's name coupled with Grace's
as the inspirer of her greatest work? For that is what will
happen — make no mistake about it. Academics, scholars,
critics, as greedy for a love interest as the most film-struck
typist, will snatch at any lubricious bits of sexuality to bring
the supreme artist down to their own pawing, clutching
level. Have we not seen Emily Dickinson bedded with a
minister and poor old Henry James doing the unmention-
able with a young sculptor? Could I not already imagine
the phrases in the literary journals: "Many of us have long
suspected that 1946 marked a climacteric in the emotional
life of Grace Eliot . . ." or "After that year a warm, roseate
streak makes its unmistakable appearance in the once cool
marble of her perfect prose . . ." or "Grace emerged from
her love affair a completed woman and a greater artist."

Ugh! Can I bear it?

But I am bitter and sour; I have to keep discounting that.
I have spent my life with authors, some of them famous, at
least two of them great, and I have not tried to ride on
their shoulders, like scholars and critics. I have given myself to them dispassionately, wholeheartedly, entering into
their very psyches; I have cajoled them, encouraged them,
edited them, supplied them with ideas in dry periods, and
even at times with story endings, and what do I have to
show for it all? A small annuity, a three-room apartment,

a life of long walks, movies and an occasional lunch or dinner with someone kind enough to remember "Old Bertie." Is there a single line about me in the multitudinous volumes of the *Dictionary of Literary Biography*? In any of the many *Who's Whos* of American letters? I have vanished like — why should I any longer even take the trouble to avoid a cliché? — like snow in springtime.

The little affair — I say little because it was of such brief duration — occurred in the spring of 1946. My first awareness of it came at a party at the Eliots' big double brownstone on Forty-eighth Street. Grace's Wednesday nights, which began at nine and ran as late as anyone cared to stay, with a constant, abundant buffet and flowing bar, represented her effort to bring those she considered "possible" or even "redeemable" in her husband's financial and social worlds together with writers and artists of the Village. As her own work was highly respected in both the milieus that she sought to mix, and as her food and liquor would have drawn the artists to the very gates of hell, she was successful. And of course, her husband had a way of putting effective pressure on any of his business associates who might have otherwise shied away from meeting "Marxists." Andy Eliot, despite Grace's perennial complaints of being "misunderstood," backed his talented wife in all her undertakings with almost too much zeal and heft.

He was a large, strong man, with a big head and small features and short, closely cropped sandy hair, who might have been almost handsome had he been a good deal less stout, and who was noisily proud of his wife. I do not suppose he could have really appreciated her books, but he was quite willing to play the devout high priest of a cult whose deity, in the holy of holies, he might never fully understand. That Grace was "too good" for him he seemed cheerfully to concede, even in the confidences he made to me, with a painful jab in my ribs, of excursions beyond the temple that need not be confided to the goddess. After all, even high priests were men.

On one such Wednesday evening, when the weather was warm and the general discussion in the parlor had abated, Grace drew me out to a corner of the garden, where we sat alone. It was known that when she so removed herself with a chosen disciple she was not to be interrupted except by the butler, who constantly replenished her glass of champagne. She was in one of her moody moods of high seriousness, and she listened pensively while I praised a group of love sonnets that she had just completed, likening them to modern-day *Sonnets from the Portuguese.*

"Well, I haven't got a poet to sweep me off to Italy," she rejoined sadly. "No, my lord and master doesn't believe that nation even exists beyond the Lido. Yet who knows? Mrs. Browning may have faced the same sort of thing. Wasn't her Robert really thinking of his next dramatic monologue while he was reading those sonnets? Did he not, if he happened upon a line superior to one of his own, die a little? Oh, husbands! What can a poor woman do but write her heart away?"

"Well, that should be enough when the writer is Grace Eliot."

"Enough? How can you say that, dear boy? Are you implying that writing is better than living? Or even a halfway substitute?"

"Of course I am. Writing is living in the highest sense."

"You really believe that? You? But how can you, when

you don't write yourself? Or *do* you? Are you a secret poet?"

"No, I don't write. It would have been my tragedy had I tried. But luckily I had the common sense to turn my frustration into a useful asset. That is why I became an agent. That is what gives me the tiny scrap of genius that I do have. It enables me to understand writers."

"But I wonder if you understand the woman under the writer." Now she put her hand to her breast with a deep sigh, trying perhaps to emulate a Mucha poster of Sarah Bernhardt as Hamlet. "Thou wouldst not think, Horatio, how ill here's about my heart — but it is no matter."

"On the contrary, it's a great matter. To me."

"Is it? I sometimes wonder how much you care about women, Bertie. I know you care about writers. I know you care about Grace Eliot. But suppose I were to tell you that Grace, the woman, has discovered something in her own heart that means more to her than any book she's ever written."

"I wouldn't believe it!" I exclaimed heatedly.

"No, you wouldn't, would you?" she responded, shaking her head. "Ah, the densities of incomprehension — the densities! To live without ever having another soul do more than brush athwart your wings in passing!"

"Who only does that, my love?" crashed in the rumbling voice of Andy Eliot, whom neither of us had noticed moving up. "Surely not your loving husband? Surely you have had more solid treatment from him?"

She gazed at his twinkling eyes without in the least changing her dreamy expression. At last she seemed to make him out, as through a mist.

"Andrew, dear, would you please tell Mercer that we

need more champagne? There's no reason that our guests should parch just because it's midnight. The Cinderellas have all gone home, and the rest of us can make merry."

Grace's mood was broken; there were no further confidences, and soon others joined us. When I was looking for my coat in the hall, I felt a hand on my shoulder, and I turned to face the tall, elegant figure of Leonard Esher, a peer in a Sargent portrait. At least he always struck me as having just changed from a scarlet huntsman's jacket.

"I say, old fellow, do you mind if I walk out with you?"

I was taken aback. Never before had Leonard done more than acknowledge my existence. Yet such is the force of a notorious snob who suddenly ceases to snub that my natural churlishness was disarmed.

"I live only three blocks from here," I heard myself saying. "I can give you a nightcap if you'd like."

"Actually, that would be perfect. I should particularly like to see your digs."

My flat, then as now, was small but cozy, with a tiny paneled library full of my collection of American firsts and some old master drawings that I had picked up as bargains. Its two windows looked north to the lights and activity of the Queensboro Bridge. Leonard stood by one of these, looking out as he sipped his cognac. I knew he would never have come up except to say something special, but that something seemed difficult for him to say.

"It's a nice place you have here, Bertie. Grace has told me about it."

"She comes here occasionally to discuss her work. I don't go to the office unless I have to. It's nicer and quieter here."

"Precisely. And Grace says she doesn't know anyone else who works at home."

"Oh?" I waited for the relevance of this.

"I'll tell you what, old boy. I'd better be blunt." Leonard turned to place his glass decisively on the table. "Grace, after all these years, has at last consented to be my mistress. You can imagine how honored and deeply affected I am."

I did not trust myself to speak. My throat felt as if a piece of iron had been crammed down it. At the moment I could only imagine that he sought to torment me. But why? Why did I, a poor worm, have to twist in the flame of their repulsive ardor?

"It has all come as a wonderful surprise to me. Years ago I had proposed it, but she had always been adamant about her duty as a wife, though God knows, Andrew has not deserved such loyalty. At length I ceased to press the matter, and we seemed to have attained a kind of platonic friendship, or *amitié amoureuse*, if you will. But now suddenly, perhaps with a sense of the passing years, Grace has seen fit to offer the gift of herself to your unworthy servant."

Was he laughing at me, the old satyr? Did he even want poor Grace now? "And where do I come in?" I gasped at last. "Why are you telling me this?"

"Ah, that's just it, isn't it? Well, you see, dear fellow, we have no place to meet. Grace would never come to my house, nor have me, for such a purpose, at hers. She is much too shy for a hotel, and she balks even at the idea of a rented flat, a 'love nest,' as she disdainfully calls it. She is morbidly afraid of discovery and says that yours is the only apartment in town that she's known to visit in the daytime."

"You mean she's safe here because people think me such a eunuch?"

Leonard dropped his eyes at this atrocious lapse of taste.

"Please, please. There is no idea of any such thing. It is simply known that your apartment is used as an office."

"And you would bring her here! While I did what? Would you have me, in Iago's phrase, 'grossly gape on' to see her topped?"

Leonard, who had just seated himself, now quickly rose. "Of course, at that I must leave. I had no idea of insulting you, nor did Grace, whose notion it was to ask you. We merely thought that, as an old and understanding friend, you might not object, on a few occasions, to using my comfortable office at the bank for a couple of hours, with my highly competent secretary and limousine thrown in. Had we known we should hurt you, the suggestion would never have been made."

"Don't go!" I cried in misery as he turned to the door. "I lost my head. Of course I'll do it; I'll be happy to do it. Tell Grace she's welcome here whenever she wishes."

"Well, that's very decent of you, I must say."

"No, no! It's decent of you to forgive my boorishness. And now we'll not speak of this again until you want the apartment. It can be ready for you any time."

Grace and I did not meet while the affair lasted; we could not have faced each other. I abominated the idea of what was going on in my poor little flat, but I will have to admit that there was never so much as a cigarette ash or an indented pillow to bring me evidence of it. After each meeting Leonard sent in a cleaning woman who left the place spotless. Yet its very shininess seemed to pollute it the more to my eyes.

Why did I mind so much? Was I in love with Grace? No, but I had made her into an idol, and I could not endure the presence of an iconoclast in her temple, particularly when this temple, this shrine, was the very home that I had dedicated to her, full of her books and manuscripts, and the rooms where she and I had worked for years over her wonderful tales. It was too horrible to think of Leonard violating her on her very altar. And this, I don't think, even in retrospect, is simply neurotic of me. I believed and still believe that the hot, rutting Grace Eliot of those fevered afternoons had no necessary relevance to the chaste goddess of letters, that Grace's genius had nothing to do with Grace's navel and that the lust of Leonard to "possess" her was his lust to bring her down to his own brute level, to prove to himself that his "creativity" was the equal of hers. And I must deny that while I live!

As I went to none of Grace's parties in these weeks and communicated with her only by letters on business matters, the end of the affair came as a complete surprise to me. As I was coming out of my building one morning I met Leonard at the door. He had been about to ring up.

"What luck, old man. I was just coming to see you. Can we walk a couple of blocks? Which way are you going?" I pointed in silence, and we fell into stride together. "I wanted to give you back your keys." I grasped these quickly as my heart soared.

"You've found a better place?" I muttered.

"We won't be needing one. *La comedia è finita.*"

A glance assured me that, if there had been any suffering, it was not registered on that craggy profile. "I hope Grace has not been hurt."

"Oh, Grace is never going to be really hurt by anything but a rash on the face or a bad book review." Here Leonard risked a sudden gesture of intimacy, rare in one so formal.

He actually put his arm around my shoulders. "Take it from me, pal: never get involved with a middle-aged virgin. They have too much to make up for."

I jerked myself free from his clutch. My astonishment was such as momentarily to stun my outrage. "How could the wife of Andrew Eliot be a virgin?"

"Oh, I don't mean a *virgo intacta*. Andrew wasn't that much of a fumbler. But the clumsy old goat could never arouse her and soon gave up trying. And after twenty years in the deep freeze poor Grace comes panting to yours truly for a bit of heaven. My God, was I ever tossed about! There were moments when I actually considered setting off your fire alarm!"

Twice I tried to speak, but no sound emerged. Was this sleazy old sport always to have the last word? Then my voice erupted.

"That lips sanctified by hers should be so foul! You great clown, don't you know you have no existence except what Grace has given you? Go down a pothole, bug."

I hurried away from him and the loud angry screech of his astonished laugh.

And now I turn again to the letters.

Oh, my lover, however little I may have given you, be assured that it was all I had. Had I been wiser I might have hoarded it and doled it out in smaller portions, but I could not do so. I opened my vault, my doors, my cupboards, my windows; I flung every gold piece and copper piece that I had at your feet. Imprudent maybe, but I care not. I shall be forever grateful. When you look with the kindly patience of an uncle whose little niece still believes in Santa Claus, I'll murmur under my breath: "Bless you for

not telling me he's a fable. Bless you for letting me pretend
a little longer."

Grace! Really!

And I must read that in the *Hamilton Review* and the
Dartington Quarterly?

Well, yes, of course I must. For I cannot destroy or even
conceal these letters. They must be entered in the record.
I have been kidding myself; I've known that all along. If
they will turn Grace Eliot's life into another of her novels,
was it not to fiction that her destiny led her? And is it not,
after all, only consistent with the justice meted out to
mortals on this planet that I, who dedicated my genius to
Grace Eliot, should have done less for her in the end than
a man who merely unzipped his fly?

The Senior Partner's Ethics

B RENDAN BROSS, Princeton '77, had intended to teach history, but after two years of graduate school he became engaged to be married, and he had to face the facts that America was an expensive place for raising families and academic jobs were in short supply. Accordingly, he abandoned his dreams of becoming the great scholar of the Byzantine empire and entered Columbia Law where, to his own surprise, he achieved high grades and an editorship of the law journal. On graduation he was offered a job in the Wall Street law firm of Nichols & Phelps, but his fiancée, who had now become a devoted social worker and a convert to Zen Buddhism, made their union contingent upon his turning down this job with "mammon." Brendan, objecting more to the imposition of the condition than to the condition itself, started work still a bachelor.

For a year this seemed just as well, for his hours were taxing. He did not mind for a time jumping into the heavy waters of bond indentures and registration statements, buffeting through days and nights and weekends the relentless breakers of galley proofs and computer printouts, because he assumed that one day he would be promoted to a position where he would be able to raise his head above the troubled surface and look over to a shore that might even contain cultural diversion, travel and, in time, a family life. But it began to strike him, as he came to know the firm better, that the intensity of industry was the same in the paneled parlor of the senior partner as it was in the whitewashed cubicle of the most junior paralegal. If there was no hell, there was also no heaven, only the endless purgatory of small print.

Well, what was wrong with that? Nothing, so long as *that* was what he wanted. But he had his doubts. Had the day passed when a man could succeed in a profession without becoming its slave? In the world where Brendan now began to think of himself as entrapped, he was borne along in the current of dedication. The men and women around him were forever droning about the number of billable hours they clocked per week. So long as they seemed doomed to be a chain gang, they must have chosen to glory in their shackles. To question the validity of a life dedicated to the apotheosis of money-making was to be guilty of heresy. So glorious indeed was the glittering gold at the apex of the corporate mountain that its mere reflection had to be reward enough for the toilers on the rocky slopes below, most of whom could not even expect to become partners of the law firms that were themselves mere handmaidens in the procession marching round and round that refulgent peak.

Or was this only Brendan's imagination? Was he losing his perspective?

A welcome change came into his life when Theodore Childe, the partner in charge of East River Trust Company, asked him to become his full-time assistant. Brendan welcomed the chance to specialize. He permitted himself to hope that once he had come to know one client and one partner intimately, there might at least be a visible constellation in that cloud-covered night sky of corporate operations.

And for some weeks, indeed, he thought he had reason to believe that he was fortunate to be working for Theodore Childe. His new boss was a straight, tall, stiff, handsome man with perfect features and a large serene brow that made his bald dome seem a crown rather than a disgrace. He was scrupulously, almost painfully neat, in his garb, in his chamber, in his very opinions. Yet he never seemed to demand an equal standard of tidiness in others. It was as if some angel or demon of his own had assigned to Theodore Childe the purely individual task of personal correctness. This might even have been, Brendan speculated, why Childe was so invariably pleasant and patient with those who worked for him. He seemed to recognize, in some curious fashion of his own, that they were not subject to the same discipline. He was almost apologetic when he corrected Brendan's work.

"There are many ways of phrasing a refunding clause," he would say, coming into his associate's office to place on his blotter a heavily blue-penciled draft on which his junior had worked a whole weekend. "I am sure that yours is as good as most, but if you don't mind looking at some of my stylistic preferences . . ."

And he would leave Brendan with an amended version of his work that represented a humiliating improvement. It was nonetheless an attractive way to be instructed, and Brendan prided himself that he responded well to it. Certainly the blue marks were soon diminishing on his drafts.

A change in his assessment of his superior was generated by the chance remark of another associate at lunch, one Jim Moher, merry, fat and (discreetly) irreverent.

"How are we getting on with Childe?" Jim asked.

"Pretty well, I guess. He seems easy enough to work with."

"Don't worry if he never gives you a compliment. That's not his way. He won't ever knock you, either. A thing is either right or it has to be done over. There's no place for praise. And none for abuse."

"Why is that?"

"Because clerks don't exist for him. They're simply tools."

"Well, he treats his tools better than some of his partners do."

"You know what the good workman doesn't blame."

"Ah, yes. It's true. He blames himself."

"Who else? There's no one but Childe in the world of Theodore Childe."

They were interrupted here by another associate who joined their table, and Brendan never asked his informant what he had meant. He knew that the latter was one of those who talked for effect, that he hated to have his ideas analyzed. Yet Brendan kept turning over in his mind Jim's loosely uttered thought in the weeks that followed. By luck or by inspiration his luncheon companion seemed to have hit upon an important aspect of Childe's personality.

When he lunched with Childe now, or when he dined, as he did on two occasions, at his dark, cold apartment, filled with heavy inherited furniture, to meet his big, hollow, uninteresting wife, Brendan noted how little change there was in the pleasant tone with which Childe dutifully

took up, one by one, the topics of general interest head-
lined in the evening paper. It was as if he were thinking:
"All right, now is the time of the social hour. In the social
hour we discuss the events of the day. When the social hour
is over we go back to work."

Did anyone exist for Childe but Childe himself? Yet the
man saw people. He saw his wife; he saw Brendan; he asked
the questions necessary to show a proper human concern.
But Brendan could not get away from an idea that now
came to dominate his thinking about his boss: that Childe's
social life was a routine that he obliged himself to go
through, that the people in it were mere characters in a
play who had had to learn their lines as he had had to learn
his. Except no — perhaps Childe was the *only* actor, and
the others marionettes whose strings were pulled by the
angel (or demon) who was composing the lines of the
comedy (or tragedy) of Theodore Childe.

Brendan lunched again with Jim Moher.

"You said none of us existed in Childe's world. Is that
even true of his family and clients?"

Jim turned out to be a less casual observer of Childe
than Brendan had supposed. He too had clerked for Brendan's boss, for several months. "I don't know so much about
his family, though I suspect the dumb, yackety wife doesn't
count for much. But the clients — or client — is another
matter. He's only got one, hasn't he?"

"Certainly only one that I've ever worked for."

"East River Trust. Natch. That's his whole life. He
grew up with the outfit. It was a small bank twenty years
ago, but it's been swelled by mergers, and he's managed each
time to hang on to the account. When they came here they
insisted the firm take him in as a partner. It was a package
deal."

"But Childe's a damn good lawyer."

Jim's mouth puckered into a circle of doubt. "He's a good enough draftsman. And he's accurate, I grant. But he's limited, specialized. If the firm ever lost that bank, they'd have no more room for Theodore Childe, and he knows it."

"But how did it all start? There must have been something in his life before East River."

Jim shrugged. "Who knows? The Childes were an old family who lost their shirts in twenty-nine. Theodore, from what I gather, grew up on handouts and scholarships in a grubby, faded-gentry kind of way. He latched on to that then-little bank as a life saver. And he's been hanging on for dear life ever since!"

Only a month after this interchange Brendan had cause to find out just how dedicated to his client Childe was. East River Trust was trustee under the will of Luke Selden, the late great pharmacist, and the trusts largely comprised stock in Selden Chemicals. To protect the trustee in its policy of keeping so many eggs in one basket — which for years had been of immense profit to the beneficiaries — East River Trust had settled its accounts judicially every five years. But at the very end of one of these periods a contraceptive pill produced by Selden had caused, or was believed to have caused, a spate of illnesses and even deaths; lawsuits had proliferated, the stock had crashed, and it was feared that the company might go into receivership. The beneficiaries of the Selden trusts, oblivious now of the vast benefits accrued to them by the policy of hanging on to the family stock, sued East River for a surcharge which, if granted, might cripple the bank.

Brendan found that once again, as before his selection by Childe, his waking hours were all devoted to his job, now the preparation of the defense. The firm's litigation department handled the court arguments and briefs, but the research was conducted by Childe and Brendan, who rapidly became experts in the science of contraception. Brendan was at first amused, then concerned and at last alarmed at the passion with which his leader attacked his task. Childe worked as long hours as his associate, tearing through files as if his very life were at stake. When he had any cause to refer to the plaintiffs or their counsel, his voice would assume a rasping bitterness.

"When you think of the years in which East River has taken such risks to enrich these useless parasites, don't you wonder that even such scabrous slugs as they are could have the gall to turn and rend their benefactor?"

"But, Mr. Childe, some of them are infants. Their guardians *have* to sue."

"Have to bite the hand that fed them? Don't give me that. And there are only two infants, anyway. How does that excuse the others?"

"Because if there *is* a surcharge, and they haven't sued, they can't share it."

"Poppycock! That's just an argument to excuse their rapacity. The kind of reasoning offered by shysters to induce greedy idiots to sue!"

Brendan did not pursue the discussion, as he could see that his superior was not quite rational on the subject, and, besides, Childe's animosity towards his opponents hardly affected the preparation of the case. But it did begin to appall him that the older man should put quite so much emotion into the fate of a bank. It was beginning to look now as if the case could probably be settled. The first flurry of motions over, there was less apparent danger that the bank would go under. Yet Childe continued to carry on as if the plaintiffs were doing something damnable in seeking redress from a trustee which had handled their portfolios in such a way as to reduce them by half.

As the days passed Brendan had even graver doubts. Was Childe's state of mind perhaps a thermometer that demonstrated how unhealthy was the moral state of the whole business world? Did these lawyers and bank officers and trust beneficiaries care about an art or a social cause or a war or a religion or even another human being as they cared about these questions of commissions and surcharges? And what was he, Brendan Bross, doing wasting his young years in other people's money battles that he did not even care about?

It was at this point, on a hot July day when the humidity outside seemed to penetrate the very ducts of the air conditioning, that Brendan came across what he was always thereafter to think of as *the* memorandum.

It recorded a discussion, at a private club in the city, between Rex Henderson, senior trust officer of East River, Theodore Childe and an economist, now deceased, one Dr. Slocum Oursley. Oursley had expressed his opinion very forcibly on the precarious nature of the drug business and the possibility of stomach poisoning from the use of certain types of vitamin pills. Attached to the memorandum was a page, written out apparently during the conference in the large handwriting of the doctor, in purple ink, giving examples of certain formulas used by Selden Chemicals that he felt to have inherent dangers. There was a third document in the file, apparently just for office purposes, signed with Childe's initials, and dated two years after the recorded discussion. It read:

Word reached us today of Dr. Oursley's suicide, apparently in a fit of depression. He is now considered discredited and has for years been fulminating against the chemical companies.

Brendan assumed that this closed the matter and that the formulas condemned by the depressed "expert" were harmless. At any rate, he did not intend to worry about them. They could wait until his opponents brought them up, which seemed unlikely. After all, his opponents were interested in contraceptives, not vitamins.

Yet only two weeks later counsel for the plaintiffs asked to examine East River's files "pertaining to a discussion of chemicals with the late Dr. Oursley." Brendan brought the request to Childe's office. The latter's answer, he thought, came just a bit too quickly.

"We never talked with Oursley. Why would we have? He was a known crank."

"But, Mr. Childe, I saw your memo about him. You met him at the Metropolitan Club."

"I don't say I didn't know the fellow. Everyone knew him. I may even have chatted with him at the Metropolitan. He was always buttonholing people. You couldn't shake him off."

Brendan still assumed that he was faced with a memory gap. "No, no, I don't mean that. I mean a serious conference with you and Mr. Henderson about the danger of certain vitamin pills."

"My dear fellow, you're dreaming."

"I'm not, sir! I can show you the file."

"Henderson would never have listened to an idiot like Oursley. And anyway, what do vitamins have to do with the price of eggs? We are dealing with contraceptives, aren't we?"

"Maybe so. Maybe the conversation was quite irrelevant. But our opponents have asked for it, and I suppose we shall have to produce it."

"If it exists."

"But I'm telling you, sir, it *does* exist. I saw it myself, only two weeks ago."

"Well, you'd better produce it, then. I'll believe it when I see it."

When Brendan returned to the conference room, which was piled high with all the files and documents of the case, and opened the box in which he was sure he had seen the memorandum, it was not there. The box was filled with correspondence, as he had remembered, but the brown folder at one end, containing only three papers and labeled "Oursley meeting," was unquestionably gone. Brendan spent the afternoon frantically searching in other similar boxes of letters, but to no avail.

When he returned to Childe's office at six, the latter had his hat on, preparing to leave for the day. Brendan fancied that he could detect a hard little gleam of hostility in those usually tranquil eyes.

"Well, Brendan?"

"I couldn't find it!"

"What couldn't you find?"

Ah, but that was wrong, that was fake! Childe always remembered everything.

"The memo about Dr. Oursley."

"Does it not occur to you, my deluded friend, that you may not have found it because you only dreamed of its existence?"

"Did I dream, too, of a paper written in purple ink, presumably by the deceased doctor, listing certain formulas used in vitamin tablets?"

"I'd be the last to deny the ingenuities of your imagination, young man."

"Mr. Childe!" Brendan exclaimed now in a stronger tone. "That document has been removed from the file. Your attitude of unreasonable disbelief makes me suspect that you know it was removed. I must ask you please to give it to me so that I may submit it to opposing counsel!"

As Childe continued to stare at him, the Indianlike cheekbones over his long pale cheeks were studded with deepening red. Brendan took in, and realized at the same time that his superior had taken in, the simple fact that Childe's failure to dismiss him from the room and possibly from the firm itself, amounted to a tacit admission of guilt. When Childe at last spoke it was almost as if he were begging for a compromise.

"And supposing it has been destroyed?" he asked. "How then should I return it?"

"*Has* it been destroyed?"

"I say supposing."

"Then that fact must be submitted to counsel and eventually, I assume, to the court. I imagine we can plead that it was due to some kind of error."

"But how will anyone ever establish what was in these 'lost' documents?"

"I presume you read them, as I did."

"But even if I had, would anyone believe me? Particularly if I testified that they were not unfavorable to my client? That they were, indeed, irrelevant to the case?"

"If they were irrelevant, why were they destroyed?"

"That is just what the jury would ask."

"Well, why were they?"

"Didn't you say yourself, it might have been a mistake?"

"*Was* it?"

"Well, supposing it was?" Childe's tone was beginning to be desperate. "Suppose they had been destroyed by mistake? Would anyone believe it? No! Look at your own face. *You* don't believe it! So that my testimony as to what was in them — or yours — would never for a minute be credited. Everyone would assume that Oursley had warned us about the contraceptive, and that we had done away with the evidence. We should have unfairly ruined our client!"

Of course this was true. Why then *had* the wretched man destroyed the file? Brendan could only suppose it was because he was afraid that a court might feel that a careful fiduciary, warned about one possible negligence, should have been alerted to the possibility of others, that defective vitamins should have put the trustee on notice of possibly defective contraceptives. Oh, no, it was absurd, and the vitamins, by all evidence, were *not* defective, and Oursley was an old fool, but Childe might have become so fanatical about his client, so terrified of its potential bankruptcy, so exhausted by the long fight, as to lose all sense of reality.

"I am sorry that should be the case," Brendan said firmly. "But it cannot alter my duty to come forward with the facts. If you will not do so, Mr. Childe, I must. I must call plaintiffs' counsel and tell them what I know. I shall probably have to tell it in court, too."

Childe's features now became contorted. He leaned over his desk, breathing hard. Brendan was afraid for a moment that he was going to vomit. But when he looked up at last, it was with a hard, contained hatred. "Do your damndest, you little swine! You're just trying to destroy me and my client. Why, I don't know, unless you're some kind of crazy radical. Just be warned, anyway, that I shall deny under oath there was ever any meeting with Oursley, or that I prepared any such memorandum. You are off the case as of this minute, and I shall suggest to our managing partner, Mr. Phelps, that you be discharged from the firm, or at least given a leave of absence on condition that you seek psychiatric help. Good day, sir!"

"Good day! Of course, I shall go immediately to Mr. Phelps myself. It is obviously my duty to offer the firm an opportunity to redress the impropriety before taking it to court. My duty not only to the firm, but to the client."

"The client!" Childe almost shrieked. "What the hell do you care about my client? Get out of here!"

Laurison Phelps dominated his great firm as few senior partners did in the 1980s, when it had become more the custom to rule by executive committee. But Phelps had some of Napoleon's superiority to delegation; his mind could cope with a problem of interoffice mail routing in the same hour that it was engaged with a brief in a multimillion dollar antitrust suit. He reveled in his own genius and versatility, and loved to astonish people with his grasp of seemingly trivial details. He was a small, shaggy man, with laughing eyes and a rasping voice that contributed all the command presence that he needed. He pretended to laugh at his own dictatorship, but it would not have been wise for anyone else to do so. His pose was one of nostalgia for a mythical past when law firms had been small bands of gifted and liberal individuals, dedicated more to their profession than to its emoluments — before, as he liked to put it, they had become "mere machines for the manufacture of fees." But woe to the associate or even partner who fell behind in that species of manufacture!

The large office in which Brendan now stood before his senior was itself designed to substantiate this pose. The walls were covered with Phelps's collection of political cartoons and engravings, going back to Nast and Daumier, most of which showed pompous and conniving attorneys in ridiculous or degrading situations. Brendan was well aware that he could not anticipate what stance Phelps would adopt even in a crisis as grave as the one he had just described. No matter how critical a matter, the senior partner could never forgo the delight of surprising his audience. Only a few months before, Brendan had witnessed Phelps's elucidation to an elderly female client of the mysteries of the generation-skipping tax. What he had outlined to the dazzled crone had not indeed been the bill passed by Congress, which Phelps had not even read, but a far better-conceived tax constructed in Phelps's fantasy on the spur of the moment! It was done, of course, more for the benefit of the listening associate than for the ignorant client. Phelps had known all the time that Brendan would follow his mental acrobatics, admire them and, when it came to drafting the required will, ignore them in favor of the actual statute that it was his more plebeian job to understand and apply.

"So, Brendan," Phelps responded now, rubbing his hands as if he and his associate were about to embark on the pleasantest of chats. "As I decline to act, you will? You are determined to strike a blow for decency and honor? I almost envy you!"

"I shall do what any lawyer in my position should do, sir."

" 'When duty calls or danger, be never wanting there!'

Of course, of course. I could argue that no matter what the truth or falsity of your charges against Mr. Childe, a paramount duty to our client prohibits a public revelation. But I admit that is questionable. So let me state again that I do not believe your charges. I do not believe for a minute that Mr. Childe destroyed that file or even that it existed. The only thing I want to do is present to you the consequences of what you are proposing to do, even under the worst assumption, i.e., that Childe is guilty. Shall I proceed?"

"Certainly, sir."

"Sit down, then, my boy, sit down." When Brendan had done so, Phelps proceeded to rub his cheeks violently, as if trying to scrub off some tightly clinging dirt. Fortunately for Brendan's ease of mind, he recognized this as an accustomed mannerism. "Have you ever stopped to observe, my friend, that when a crime is committed by an amateur, it is — nine times out of ten — an unnecessary crime? That it is usually, in fact, the one event bound to bring on the very catastrophe it was designed to avoid?"

"I don't know that I follow you, sir."

"Richard Nixon destroyed his presidency by unlawfully covering up an episode that, let alone, would have proved at most a temporary embarrassment. Richard Whitney, a Stock Exchange president, was jailed for embezzling three relatively small sums of money, without which the house of Morgan would have bailed him out of all his financial troubles."

Brendan continued to stare at this glibly talking little man. "How am I to relate this to what Mr. Childe has done?"

"Very simply. Childe, according to you, has destroyed evidence which, introduced in court, would not have substantially strengthened the plaintiffs' case. But when the jury finds that it has been done away with, it will blacken the defendant in its eyes. It will result, if not in a plaintiffs' victory, at least in a settlement less advantageous to our client than could have been otherwise obtained. Poor Childe will have placed a gun to the temple of his cherished bank and pulled the trigger. You will see now what I mean by the folly of the amateur in crime. By his own act Childe will have brought on precisely what he has most sought to avert. Is it any wonder that some psychiatrists saw an element of the suicidal in what Nixon did?"

"Do you imply the same of Mr. Childe?"

"Well, he will have certainly achieved his own ruin. *If* he destroyed that file. And wasn't there something seemingly deliberate in the way he left the evidence for you to discover? If, of course, he left it?"

As Brendan stared at the senior partner he began to wonder if the whole thing were not to Phelps simply a fascinating drama, an enthralling case history. Could detachment be carried further? Or was it voyeurism, so long as Phelps himself preferred psychiatric terms? Had he not just virtually admitted that he believed his partner guilty?

"Let me consider first the results of your acting as you propose," Phelps continued. "And secondly those of your not doing so. After the court has received your information, our client will certainly discharge us as counsel. The firm will be tarnished, but not destroyed. One can live anything down these days — in time. Except for Childe himself, who may be disbarred, if your testimony is believed. His life, we must presume, will be ruined. As for East River Trust, it will be obliged, as I have already indicated, to seek a settlement considerably harsher than it deserves. And what are the social goals to be anticipated from your noble conduct? Is a criminal punished? But surely poor Childe, if guilty, could not suffer much more than he must be suffering now. Very well, what about deterrence? Will Brendan Bross's gesture have prevented a further crime by Childe? Hardly. For even if Childe did what you suppose, it is obviously a once-in-a-lifetime felony, and he will have been too scared by the confrontation you've already had with him to try the like again. So now let us consider the scenario where Brendan Bross decides to take no further step with respect to the supposedly suppressed evidence."

"You mean where I fail my duty to the bar?"

"We are speaking hypothetically, sir." For the first time there was a hint of sharpness in the senior partner's tone. "Allow me, if you will, to finish. The litigation comes to its proper conclusion, with a settlement satisfactory to our client and in keeping, I must insist, with the best economic interests of the community. Our distinguished law firm continues its distinguished career, minus one partner who, if actually guilty, will probably soon elect a quiet retirement. And Brendan Bross . . ."

Here Phelps paused, contemplating his associate with twinkling eyes. Brendan's heart swelled with a sudden spurt of satisfaction and anger as he thought he spotted the game.

"And Brendan Bross becomes a junior partner!" he cried.

Phelps's explosive laughter seemed to carry a note of triumph. "Ah, dear fellow, you can't really think me such an ass as that! To *push* you into rushing to the judge with the last smitch of doubt removed from your fatuous heroism? Oh, no, my friend, I shan't help you like *that*. The moral choice is yours and yours alone. You will have no idea how your acting or not acting will affect your future in this firm. You will have no idea because *I* have no idea. *I* shall not speak of your memorandum to our opponents because I do not believe it existed. *You* do, so you have the problem. How you solve it is up to your own conscience."

"But —"

"Good day, sir!"

Brendan wondered afterwards, alone in his office, his throbbing head in his hands, if the old ham actor really got a kick out of anything but his own performances.

The next day Brendan conferred with plaintiffs' counsel, and the day after that he was interrogated in court about the lost memorandum. His firm promptly took him off the case, but he was not discharged. However, when on the afternoon after his testimony he returned to the office none of the partners or associates did more than coldly nod to him in the passageways. Nobody crossed his threshold. He was obviously regarded as a dangerous lunatic.

Their attitude changed, however, when Mr. Henderson of East River was called. He was the trust officer who, according to the memorandum, had been present at the conference at the Metropolitan Club with Childe and Oursley. He made a nervous and stammering witness, but under relentless examination he at last confirmed that the conference had indeed been held, that Oursley had indeed made notes in purple ink which he handed to Childe, and that Childe had told Henderson he would send him a memo of the meeting but never had.

A newspaper article the next day raised the question of disbarment proceedings against Theodore Childe. The following morning at six a.m. Childe jumped from a bathroom window of his apartment and fell ten stories to the pavement.

In the ultimate settlement of the suit against East River Trust the general opinion was that the undiscovered memorandum about the vitamin pills had been of little or no importance.

Brendan, propped up in his bed in his bare single room at the psychiatric division of the Yorkville Hospital, kept his head turned away from the neat pile of untouched books and magazines on his table and maintained his steady gaze over the sluggish river and the rapidly moving craft that plied their accustomed way up and down it. He was well enough now to go out once a day and trudge along the pedestrians' walk without anyone's fearing that he might try to jump in.

He was also well enough to have visitors, and he had one now in the person of none less than the senior partner of the law firm with which he was not sure that he was still associated.

Mr. Phelps, perhaps having been instructed by the nurse to discourse on neutral topics, was holding forth, a bit fatiguingly, on the ludicrous minor details of a vast antitrust suit in which the firm was engaged. But suddenly he stopped. Suddenly he blustered his way boldly into an area that he must surely have been warned away from.

"When I was young my mother suffered from depressions. I used to wonder why she couldn't pull herself together. Why she didn't simply snap out of it. I suppose children are inclined to be unsympathetic. I've always had to watch my step with depressed people since."

Brendan smiled. "That sounds more as if you were trying shock treatment."

"Well, I don't believe you're really depressed. In the medical sense, anyway. You have what is called a 'real' worry. You blame yourself for Childe's death."

"Don't you blame me? Didn't you as much as warn me?"

"Perhaps. But you did what you had to do. The fact that Childe died of it has nothing to do with your duty. He chose to die. If a man elects to do what *he* did and then prefers to die rather than face the consequences, why is that a thing for you to worry about?"

Brendan took in, wonderingly, the other's matter-of-fact expression. "But suppose, sir, I was not motivated by duty? Suppose I was venting my spleen against the whole world of law? Suppose I wanted to make an issue of my disgust at seeing the best lawyers of the land dedicate their talents and morals to the simple business of oiling the machinery of money-grabbing? Suppose I wanted to see Theodore Childe's head tumble into the basket, like a *tricoteuse* in the French Revolution?" Brendan's voice rose to a high note, but it occurred to him that he was forcing it, and he at once became silent. Was he trying to convince Phelps that he *was* ill? Was he trying to convince himself?

"What does it matter what your motives were? What you did you had to do. Your thought processes and your act were two distinct and independent things. Suppose in your mind you want to kill John Jones. But you don't do so. You don't even show him your animosity. And then suppose John Jones goes berserk and hijacks a school bus and you're a cop and have to kill him to save the kids. Does it matter that you wanted to do it anyway?"

"It seems to me, sir," Brendan said slowly, keeping a

grave eye on Phelps, "that you're begging the whole question. You say I *had* to do what I did. But did I? Would you have done it?"

"Certainly, in your situation."

"You astound me. I thought you were advising me not to do it on that day when I consulted you."

"I was simply analyzing the situation. I was not in your shoes. You will recall that I told you I did not believe that Childe had destroyed that memorandum."

"But that wasn't true. You *did* believe it."

Phelps met Brendan's stare without flinching. Then he chuckled. "All right, yes. We both know I did."

"Then why were you not in my shoes?"

"Because I hadn't, like you, *seen* the memorandum. I had only your word for it."

"But you believed my word."

"That is a purely subjective matter. Did I have a right to believe it? Was it reasonable for me to take the word of an associate I hardly knew against that of a partner whom I had known and trusted for twenty years? Was that doing my duty to a client? Oh, no, my friend, I did not have the presumption to substitute my inner hunch of what had really happened for the presumption of right conduct that my partner surely deserved."

"So that is the law," Brendan mused. "And if you had been I and had seen the memorandum you would have done as I did?"

"Precisely."

"And yet you tried to talk me out of it!"

"Well, you see, it wasn't *my* duty to do it. It was my duty to my client to avoid, if possible, the whole bloody mess."

"Even at the price of talking me out of doing *my* duty?"

"Well, if you were weak-minded, didn't I owe it to East River Trust to work on your weak mind?"

"Good God, could things be that simple?"

"It makes life easier to live, doesn't it? And isn't life hard enough without making it harder? When will you be coming back to work, Brendan?"

"You mean you want me to?"

"Why not? Everyone admires you for your guts. East River fired us, as you know, but they're not too displeased with the outcome of the case, and I think they're beginning to realize that Childe's act hadn't hurt them as much as they thought it had. It's true they panicked and lost a few points in the settlement, but that was their fault. They may come back to us, now that Childe is gone. And if they don't, hell, there are other banks. And the world has a very short memory."

"But even if that is so, what about all I've told you about what I think of the practice of law?"

"Oh, that." Phelps rose now, as if ready to conclude his visit. "Well, that's the way I feel about it myself. Come, Brendan, you and I didn't make the world."

And Brendan, left alone, gazed again out his window at the dirty gray of the rippling river under the serene blue of the early spring sky and wondered if all his fears and fancies did not belong to an episode in a television ghost series. Were they simply his "twilight zone"? But even if they were, might they not be preferable to the bleak realism of the senior partner? Brendan's trouble — oh, how he saw it now! — was that he had nothing to combat that realism with.

The Takeover

I FIRST MET Peter Chisholm in the winter of 1981 when we were both single men, considerably in view on the Manhattan social scene, both in our late forties, he divorced and I separated. But that was the extent of our greatest common denominator. In all other points we were near opposites. I was a native-born New Yorker, of staidly respectable New England antecedents, while his were undisclosed. Lithuanian? Jewish? A touch of the Tatar? All we knew of his background was that he had attended high school in Hoboken. But if his social and ethnic origins were shadowy, his present was nonetheless glittering. While I labored in a small art gallery on Madison Avenue in which I had purchased an even smaller interest with my whole inheritance, he was the leading partner in a firm of investment bankers and known throughout town as the "avenging angel" of the corporate takeover.

His appearance proclaimed his formidability. He was stocky and muscular, if on the short side, with bulging shoulders, a square face with distrustful little green eyes and thick, short, stubby yellow hair. His voice, however, was mild, almost velvety, faintly mocking, guardedly friendly. He never seemed to raise it or to lose his equanimity. His anger, if anger he ever felt, was expressed in quick snorts of laughter.

Since his divorce, some years back, from a woman whom none of my friends seem to have known, he lived in a large penthouse on Central Park West filled with the eclectic collection of art that evidenced the constant changes of his taste. It was through this collection that we had become friends — if such a term could describe any relationship with Peter. The only reason that, as a dealer, I survived his fickleness was that my gallery covered a wide range of artifacts. Peter would pace up and down the main showroom with curiosity and suspicion. Was it all just so much wallpaper? Or was it a business to take over?

"What is this?" he asked me once, pointing to the portrait of a lady in a straight, white, high-necked gown with a turban.

"A Vigée-Lebrun. And a very fine one. Just the thing to go in your dining room over the George II silver."

"You really think she's my sort of picture?"

"Why not? Isn't she graceful?"

"Don't I need something sweller?"

"Sweller? She's a grand duchess."

"You mean a Russian? Why would a French painter have done a grand duchess?"

"Because Madame Vigée-Lebrun, very sensibly, emigrated from France during the revolution and went to Moscow where she made a fortune painting the imperial court. She must have been a kind of female Peter Chisholm."

He eyed the portrait now with greater respect. But then he sniffed: "I'll bet she's out of fashion. Would Meyer Shapiro approve of Vigée-Lebrun?"

"I doubt she's his affair. Should I care about that? We

dealers know that fashion is king. Vigée-Lebrun was fashionable once. She'll come back. Everything comes back. Everything, that is, with some basic artistic merit."

"How do you spot that?"

"Ah, that's a dealer's eye."

"And you have it?"

"I have a bit of it. If a picture catches my fancy, I don't stop to write an essay on why. I make a bid. Maybe it's a Bouguereau. Or an Alma-Tadema. Or a Kandinsky. Or a Cy Twombly. I don't care. Does it speak to me? That's all I ask. And the only other principle is never to dump. That's what warehouses are for. If it hit your eye once, it may hit it again. Hang on to it!"

"Are you making a fortune? Like Vigée — whatever her name is?"

"Well, I might if I owned more of this shop. But I have only a very small share."

"Maybe I should invest in it," Peter said thoughtfully.

It was on another of these visits that Peter met my wife, with whom I had remained on friendly terms. Abby used to drop into the gallery at times when there were apt to be no customers, or only "browsers," at, say, ten o'clock in the morning, and she would sit on the edge of my desk, smoking, swinging one of her long legs, the absurdly high heel of her slipper tapping against its side, her long blond hair falling across her cheek as she voiced her sharp, terse opinions on everything and everyone. Abby represented a rather rickety bridge between a generation of New York women that was still content with society and social work and one that was concerned with jobs and professions. She was bored with social life and at the same time irritated that her juniors had ceased to take it seriously. She was too old and too lazy to learn a profession, and she liked to imagine that she had wasted the best years of her life trying to make a home for me, which was absurd, as I had always been perfectly content with my books and gallery. Of course I was egocentric and selfish myself, but certainly no more so than she. I had created my own happiness. Why couldn't she?

No sooner had I introduced Peter than they struck up a kind of humorous alliance against myself. He pointed to a painting of a French interior that I had placed on an easel for his better perusal.

"Your husband, Mrs. Day, thinks I should buy this. No doubt he brought it down from the attic when he suspected I'd be dropping in. Don't you think it has a kind of attic look?"

Abby took in the viewer appraisingly before she turned to the canvas. It was obvious that she was interested in Peter; women usually were. She glanced briefly at the quiet Gallic salon with its gray panels, its commode and bergères, and the window opening to the edge of a formal garden.

"Well, if you like Walter Gay," she said with a shrug.

"Oh, you knew it was a Walter Gay. Tell me about Walter Gay."

"He did his friends' châteaux, as you see. He was one of those exquisite expatriates of Edith Wharton's world. He could paint, I admit. Lucian likes his things because there are no people in them. You don't even feel that anyone's just left the room. They are totally empty. Voids."

"Is that it, Lucian? You don't like people?"

Well, I could play their silly game as well as they. "I don't especially like the people who occupied Gay's rooms, no. Marquis and comtes with rich American wives. But the rooms, at least, are beautiful. Gay believed that rooms have souls even if their owners don't. Or perhaps he imagined the souls the occupants thought they might develop by living in those rooms."

"As Lucian hopes to be saved by surrounding himself with gewgaws," Abby drawled, getting up to display her figure in strolling before this new prey. "He thinks there may be some kind of spiritual osmosis from old prints and vases."

"What do you think I should buy, Mrs. Day?"

"Call me Abby, for goodness' sake. What should you buy? Let me see." She looked him up and down as if she were measuring him for a suit. Then she strode down the gallery to a cabinet of precious metals. "I know what you should buy." She picked up a small lion, flattened to be worn as a pin or buckle. "Scythian gold! Made by some wretched Greek slave for a pirate's hoard. Or maybe for his tomb where he would be buried with cattle and horses and wives, all walled up alive with his jewel-decked corpse!" She crossed the room to hold the lion against Peter's chest. "Yes, that's it. You should have an apartment with dark paneling and nothing on the cabinet shelves but objects of refulgent gold. And they should all be loot, too!"

It irritated me to see how obviously Peter was enjoying her crude flattery, and I tried to end this absurd discussion by taking the Scythian lion from Abby and putting it back on the shelf. But when I turned I found them ready to leave — together.

Things between those two went rapidly; it was an obvious case of symbiosis. Abby wanted Peter's money and power, and he wanted her elegance and style. The sexual game between them was equally obvious: she was playing the haughty Roman princess who yearns to be raped by the barbarian, and he was Attila, titillated by her degrading urges and thrilled by his own brutishness. But it would have been petty on my part to begrudge Abby her little triumph. She had not, after all, had much from our childless marriage, and I should have been glad to see her better herself so long as not at the expense of someone to whom I owed a duty. What possible duty could I owe to Peter Chisholm?

And so when she dropped into the gallery one morning, looking particularly smug, I remarked with heavy joviality: "Well, is he on the hook now? Are you ready for the net?"

Abby seemed actually embarrassed. "Well, I'm beginning to think he really likes me."

"You mean what Tennessee Williams calls a letch or the real thing?"

"Oh, the real thing — what rot you talk, Lucian. I mean I think I can marry him."

"And that's what you want?"

"Well, shouldn't I? I mean, isn't he about the hottest thing in his field?"

"Would that make him the hottest thing in your bed?"

She shrugged. "I haven't been fool enough to give him the chance to show me, anyway. But what the hell, he's not a fag, is he? Wasn't there a first wife and kids?"

"Oh, I don't mean he isn't manly enough for all reasonable women. But are you that, darling? You weren't always."

"That's right; blame me and not your own tepid ardor. But I don't want to get into all that again, for Christ's sake. I want your help, Lucian."

"All right."

She looked at me doubtfully. "Seriously?"

"Of course."

"Well, then, I want you to make him think we've been considering a reconciliation."

I stared. "You mean you want to move back? But you can't! My apartment's too small."

"No, no, that won't be necessary. We'd only have to be seen dining together. Or going to people's houses together. We could let it be known that we'd dropped the idea of getting a divorce."

"And why, pray, would we do this?"

"To fool Peter." She suddenly became excited. "You see, Lucian, Peter never really wants anything unless it belongs to somebody else. He can't be aroused unless he's grabbing it from someone who values it."

"You make him sound charming."

"Never mind that. That's what they call the 'given.' That's where we start. Oh, Lucian, if you wreck this for me, you really will be a bastard. Give me my chance, will you? I promise that once I'm Mrs. Peter Chisholm I'll buy out your whole gallery. And if it's him you're worried about, damn it all, I'll make him a perfectly good wife. As good a wife as he'll be a husband, anyway."

As I stared at the yellow gleam in Abby's now desperate eyes I wondered if this were simply the case of her last chance for a money match or whether she might conceivably have lost what scrap of a heart she possessed to our new tycoon. But in either event she was right. I owed her a boost.

It was not long after my reluctant promise to play this rather ignoble role that Peter came into the shop to check up on me. He did not beat around the bush.

"Are you and Abby thinking of getting together again?"

"I don't suppose I'm required to answer that."

"Well, don't you think you should? How's a guy like me to know if the road is clear?"

"A guy like you? I didn't realize there were guys like you, Peter."

"Me, then. I haven't been able to figure out whether or not this is a 'hostile' takeover."

"You're sure it *is* a takeover?"

"Of course I am. I want Abby. The point is: do you?"

His directness made it hard for me. I had not anticipated that he would play so fair. But a promise is a promise, and I could not give Abby away. "I don't think I care to discuss my relationship with my wife with anyone but her."

"But I'm telling you. I want her!"

"And do you suppose that entitles you to her? Do you think you can just grab anything in this life you want?"

"I trade; I don't grab," he corrected me. "I give full value for what I get. That's what life is, trading or fighting. Take your pick. It's the soldiers, not the merchants, who cause all the trouble."

"Why do you look at me like that? Aren't I a merchant, too? I certainly don't feel like a soldier."

"Any more than you act like one!" Peter exclaimed with a rude laugh. "Yes, I suppose you are a petty trader — in dolls' houses. Your trouble is that, coming from a so-called old family, you inherit the soldier's silly code of honor, which is nothing but a kind of etiquette between massacres. But honor or no honor, I repeat: do you want Abby?"

"Do you care whether or not I do?"

He looked at me hard for a moment and then shrugged. "No, I don't suppose I do. Now."

"Well, if you think I'm going to sign her over to you by a conveyance, you are quite wrong."

I was not very happy at how I had conducted myself, but Abby seemed content. Not long after this her lawyer called me up to arrange for a friendly divorce; it appeared that the mighty Chisholm was actually committing himself. There seemed to be only one hitch; his insistence on a prenuptial agreement. Abby seemed to regard this as an infringement of her fundamental rights as a free white American fortune hunter.

"But isn't he settling something on you?" I asked when she burst into my gallery to complain·about it.

"A measly hundred G's! And do you know what he wants in return? He wants me to waive every right I have to every penny of his fortune! Even on a divorce. Even on his death!"

"He could still provide for you in his will."

"But how can I count on that? Did you ever hear anything so chintzy?" She shrugged angrily when she saw my smile. "Oh, I know. You think I have a hell of a nerve to object, considering it's the money I'm after. But that's all a matter of motive. That will soon be in the past. This is a marriage we're talking about, which will soon be the *present*. A man has certain obligations in a marriage."

"I thought it was divorce we were really talking about."

"Well, that's part of marriage, isn't it? Suppose five years from now, he decides to kick me out. How am I supposed to support myself?"

"On your settlement, I presume."

"But I can't live on *that*. And I'll be older. It may not be that easy to snag another guy."

"Oh, I'll be around."

"Thanks! I've got to have better security than that. Seriously, Lucian, what should I do?"

"Sign the agreement. It won't stand up in a court of law. You'll be the helpless little girl who knew nothing about business and was so much in love she signed what the big bad wolf put before her. Why, it's a pushover! Chisholm won't have a chance with a jury."

"Are you sure of that?"

"Well, I can't guarantee it, but I'd give strong odds. Anyway, one thing *you* can be sure of is that you'll scare him off for good if you refuse to sign."

"Can't I make a scene about its not being a thing he can ask of a lady?"

"Haven't you done that already?"

"I suppose so." Poor Abby seemed to droop. "I guess you're right. There's no other way to play it. And I thought the law favored us poor girls. I should have known it was made by chauvinist pigs."

Once Abby had agreed to sign the prenuptial agreement, it was only a matter of days before she became Mrs. Peter Chisholm. In the year that followed I did not see much of the newlyweds, who moved in circles more exclusively financial than mine, but I followed the course of their social life in the public prints. Abby received wide coverage, and her photograph showed her among the high and mighty in the world of the charity ball. With her looks and social energy and Peter's dynamism and gold, they became almost overnight one of the most fashionable couples in town.

My first indication of trouble even in that paradise came one night at a dinner party when I was seated by Abby. It chastened my ego to realize that our hostess did not even know that I had been married to her. Abby, in her usual way, picked me up just where she had left me.

"You're looking for Peter," she observed as my eye ran over the room. "He's not here. He's working. He gave out at the last moment. He does that whenever he likes."

"Well, at least he works to good purpose. When I worked at night it wasn't to provide you with ruby bracelets like that one."

"But he's always grinding. I thought we'd be able to travel and do all sorts of things. He used to sneer at people who talked about how hard they worked. He said it was a rotten American habit."

"Talking about it. Not doing it."

"Well, he took me in completely. I thought he was a genius who could pull off a deal by noon and then take me to the races. That was the way *he* talked, anyway. And now what do I find? That he works like a nigger!"

A month later, when I met Abby at a cocktail party, again without her husband, she looked even more plainly discontented.

"Do you know what he's just done? He's bought a château in the Dordogne! Without so much as a pretty please."

"How charming! I'd love to have a château in the Dordogne."

"But it's nowhere near anyone that I know. I'm not going to hole up in some French province every summer. Besides, it's hot as Hades there."

"What does he say when you tell him that?"

"He says I don't have to come. He consults me in nothing! The apartment is run by his butler. The meals are all ordered and prepared by the cook. He draws up the dinner lists. I might be a guest in my own home!"

"But doesn't he let you buy what you want?"

"Oh, he gives me money. That's not a problem. He's even offered to buy the floor beneath us so I could furnish that the way I wanted. But *his* things, *his* life can't be touched. It's crazy. No husband's like that. No American husband, anyway."

"My advice to you, Abby, is to settle down and accept it. You've got what you were after. Don't rock the boat."

But Abby was utterly incapable of such resolution. She suffered from a sense of personal outrage over Peter's refusal to give her a seat on the board of directors of his existence. She beat her fists in vain against the adamantine wall of his will. I had not realized how strongly she felt about what she called "principles." She seemed to feel that she was letting down her whole sex in allowing Peter to dominate the home as well as the office. If need be, she might even prove a martyr!

I realized how serious things were when she asked me to lunch at her apartment, and arriving, found there were just the two of us. Abby's tone was clipped and hard.

"I thought as my 'ex' you'd be interested to know that I'm planning to move Peter into your category. But he is certainly being very difficult. He won't give me a penny! Before I talk to my lawyers I want to ask your opinion. Didn't you once tell me that prenuptial agreement would never stand up in court?"

"Not if you have grounds for divorce."

"But it seems I haven't! That's what Peter blandly assures me. Nor will he give me any. He looks at me in that maddening way, and says, 'Lady, face it. You're stuck.' "

"Could I have a look at that agreement?"

We went into the library to see the papers, and I admit that I was appalled to see what she had signed. There were two large bound volumes of typed inventory listing not only every stock, bond, mortgage or other security that Peter owned, but every partnership or joint venture in which he had a minor interest, and every item of tangible personal property down to his last pair of cuff links. And Abby had affixed her initials to every single page! The agreement itself was equally detailed, containing lengthy descriptions of Peter's broad commercial ambitions and promises on Abby's part not to look beyond what he would provide for her in his will, even should his estate exceed a hundred million dollars.

"But this is ridiculous!" I exclaimed. "Even if you can't get a settlement, you're still entitled to alimony."

"How do I get alimony if I can't get a divorce? Or even a separation? I have to have grounds, Lucian!"

"But I thought any grounds would do these days. I thought if your husband trumped your ace in bridge it was cruel and inhuman treatment."

"But the bastard won't trump my ace! He's a goddamn model husband!"

It was only a week after this — for everything went rapidly where Peter was concerned — that he came to see me at my gallery. "My" gallery! I was at once to be disillusioned about that.

"You're going to be working for me from now on, Lucian," he said in his velvet tone, eyeing me with wry amusement. "I've bought out the major interest in this gallery."

"So? You'll make an art fortune now?"

"With any luck and your assistance. Would you like to know my reasons for doing it?"

"I don't suppose you have to tell me."

"Any more than you had to tell me about the true nature of your relationship with Abby?"

I felt a chill of apprehension at the flicker in those green eyes. "You mean our pretending that we might be reconciled? I'm not very proud of that."

"It was a shabby trick. And it didn't work, because I wasn't in the least interested in taking anything away from you. I wanted Abby for exactly the use she has been to me. In my bed and at my board. And I intend now to avail myself of just what I need from you."

"I don't see what good I can be to you. Or Abby either now, for that matter."

"I still need Abby, at least as my hostess. We met this morning with her lawyer, and she gave up the idea of a divorce. It came hard, but she did. She saw that she was licked about the money, and, deep down, she knows she's too old and too disagreeable to catch another fat cat. I think she learned a little about reality this morning."

"Poor Abby!" I saw her in his pincers, wriggling. But hadn't she asked for it? Then I had a sudden tremor of outrage at all he took for granted. "Don't forget, Chisholm, she'll be watching you. The first misstep —"

"There won't be any misstep. With my kind of dough all tracks can be covered."

"There will, then, be tracks?"

"Do you think I'd tell you?"

"What, then, do you want of me?"

"I want you to drop everything and put together a collection of Scythian gold. If you have to rob the Hermitage in Leningrad!"

And looking at that mocking glare I thought of the great cave of a tomb that poor Abby had described, with the body of Peter decked out in gorgeous gems and myself frantically decorating the chamber with golden images, hoping that the eagle-faced guards would let me out before they rolled the giant stone into the entranceway, but reading at last my fate in the terrified eyes of the one who was doomed to share it.